CHALKLINE

CHALKLINE

jane mitchell

WALKER
BOOKS

First published in Great Britain 2009 by Walker Books Ltd
87 Vauxhall Walk, London SE11 5HJ

2 4 6 8 10 9 7 5 3 1

Text © 2009 Jane Mitchell

Cover images:
Boy © 2009 Plush Studios/Photolibrary
Background © 2009 Nonstock/Photolibrary

The right of Jane Mitchell to be identified as author of this
work has been asserted by her in accordance with the
Copyright, Designs and Patents Act 1988

This book has been typeset in Fairfield

Printed in Great Britain by Clays Ltd, St Ives plc

British Library Cataloguing in Publication Data:
a catalogue record for this book is
available from the British Library

ISBN 978-1-4063-1517-2

www.walker.co.uk

In memory of Sandy W,
who never got to see the end

PROLOGUE

Rafiq tightened the orange bandanna around his face and crouched low behind the rocks. Drawing his assault rifle to eye level, he peered down the length of its barrel and trained his sight on the highway below. He could see the dusty road from where it twisted upwards from the town of Poonch, curving against the flank of the mountain, to where it disappeared at the hairpin bend leading to the Haji Pir pass, eventually snaking across the border into Pakistan. The morning sun was cresting the distant peaks, blessing the cold blueness of the sky with a soft light. At this early hour the road was empty.

Tariq, a younger boy, lay prone beside him, his gun also at the ready.

"This is a good spot," he whispered to Rafiq, glancing at his mentor. "We can see everything, yet they won't see us at all."

Rafiq didn't take his eyes from the road as he answered the twelve-year-old. "That's why I chose it. Keep your eyes on the road, Tariq. There should be no idle talk at times like this."

The boy's face reddened and he immediately turned back to his gun.

Rafiq rested his rifle down and looked at Omar, the other boy with them. He was focused on the road. Not a muscle twitched and his eyes barely blinked lest he miss any movement.

"Can you see the other fire team?" Rafiq asked.

Omar wondered if this was a test of his skills, or a task that Rafiq was about to ask him to do. It was difficult to tell with Rafiq. Omar moved only his eyes, keeping his head low, and checked out the rough scattering of rocks and shale on the far side of the road. He could just see the others: dark heads silhouetted, the glint of the rising sun on the barrels of three rifles.

"I can see where they are."

"Can you shoot them from here?"

Omar hesitated and blinked. "I think so."

"Then they are too exposed. Learn this lesson: if you can kill them, then so can the enemy. Tell them afterwards and keep yourself hidden from view."

Relieved, Omar returned his gaze to the empty road. Rafiq took up his gun again and lay low, feeling the hard pebbles against his stomach. Even when he squinted in the new light, he was unable to see where they had laid the mines. That was good. It was the way it should be.

Under cover of darkness they had crept along this exact stretch of road, digging shallow holes in the ruts left by passing vehicles and carefully placing explosives. It was the first proper mission for the younger boys and they had been nervous and excited.

"Don't allow your hands to shake when you arm the explosives," Rafiq warned them, squatting down to examine their work.

"I can't help it. They shake no matter what I do," replied Omar.

"Control them." Rafiq's command was sharp. "Otherwise we'll be blown to bits and our mission will be a failure."

Omar wiped his sticky palms on his shirt and inhaled deeply. It was easier when Rafiq wasn't breathing down his neck. Although he was only two years older, Rafiq's demeanour was more like an adult's.

"How far apart should they be?" Rafiq asked.

"Twenty-five paces ahead of the main formation." Omar's teeth chattered in spite of himself. Nights in the high peaks were bitterly cold and his thin shirt held little warmth. "And ten paces apart."

Rafiq nodded briefly.

The boys flitted like small spirits in the moonlight until their tasks were complete and Rafiq was satisfied. Once the mines were armed, they scooped dirt over the holes and scattered twigs and stones to conceal where the road had been dug.

"It's nearly dawn," Rafiq told the group. "Not much longer to wait. Go to the ambush points and stay hidden until the convoy arrives. It should be here shortly after sunrise."

As they retreated, they swept branches over the dusty road to conceal their footprints. The group split and hid among the rocks on either side of the road. Rafiq was accustomed to concentrating solely on the task ahead. He scarcely noticed the cold or the rumblings of his empty belly as he spent the waiting hours thinking through the mission and praying for success.

Slowly the hills took shape as the light shifted from cold blue to dawn. The boys were grateful to feel the early rays of the sun warm their bones. When the air was bright, they pulled their bandannas over their young faces. As expected, the roar of motorbikes soon filled the air and a thick cloud of dust at the hairpin signalled the approach of the convoy. Vehicles came into view: four motorbikes in front, a sleek black car and an armed personnel carrier with a mounted machine gun on top. The boys ducked low and waited. The leading motorbikes rolled harmlessly over the anti-tank mines. The car followed, bumping along the ruts on the road, its wheels dipping deeply into the freshly dug earth.

Everything happened at once.

The quiet morning smashed to pieces as sharp explosions rent the air. The car lurched off the road and pitched upwards, doors flying off, wheels spinning along the road. It crashed down with a dull explosive sound. The ruined

vehicle sank low. At the same time, the motorbikes detonated the lighter, sensitive mines. Dirt, black smoke and
bikes fountained high into the air, slamming the riders
back onto the hard road. Their bikes crashed on top of
them. The personnel carrier at the rear braked sharply. Its
back doors flew open, spilling armed guards out like angry
ants. Some ran to the car; others took up defensive positions on the ground.

The stillness was shattered by the deafening frenzy
of guns and explosions, men shouting and the grinding of
metal. The machine-gunner twisted his weapon around
wildly, firing into the hills but not knowing where to shoot,
or even if anyone was there to shoot at. Rafiq and the boys
covered their heads as rocks splintered and exploded close
to where they hid, showering them with grit and rubble.

After the initial explosions and panic, and when there
was no counter-attack, the army ceased firing. The soldiers paused to see what would happen next. They waited in uneasy silence, nerves singing, ears ringing, as they
strained to catch the sound of any movement, wide eyes
searching the hills surrounding them. Perhaps there was
no one out there. Perhaps after the mines had been laid
the enemy had retreated.

Nothing stirred. No click of rolling rocks betrayed a
hidden sniper. There was no flash of a gun barrel or flutter
of a shirt. The brown hills seemed empty of life.

Cautiously the soldiers moved forward, edging along
the side of the personnel carrier and creeping towards the

car. Still nobody shot at them. Two soldiers ran up to the motorbike riders, who were lying broken and injured on the road, and hid behind the wrecked bikes. Their eyes darted nervously to the watching hills as they dragged their comrades from beneath the smashed-up machines. They stayed low and ran to the gaping sides of the car, pulling out smoking bodies.

From his hiding place Rafiq watched with contempt the actions of these foolish men. Did they really believe that there was nobody waiting for them? When the soldiers were no longer in organized formation but scattered and vulnerable, Rafiq gave the signal. His ambush teams started firing. Cold and unflinching, the six children picked off the army personnel one by one.

When the firing stopped and the dust and smoke had cleared, bodies were scattered on the ground. Rafiq and his teams stayed hidden, but studied the area with care. Any one soldier left alive could annihilate them; a sniper after an ambush was the most dangerous, because he'd be cornered, frightened and vicious. Rafiq's sharp eyes darted to a sudden movement behind one of the bikes, but it was only the torn shirt of a biker flapping in the breeze.

From the other side of the road Ahmed looked across at him. His two boys were motionless behind their guns, their eyes glued to the site of the ambush. They waited for Rafiq to give the all-clear, then descended warily to the road, approaching the blown-up vehicles cautiously. The boys scurried around, counting the bodies and checking they were dead. Some of the soldiers were young, and their lifeless eyes stared at the children who had murdered them.

Rafiq snapped out orders. "Gather all weaponry: unused grenades, rifles, handguns. Take the magazines from the machine gun. Check for extra weapons in the personnel carrier and test the mines we laid. Disarm any unexploded arsenal and take it back to camp. Collect documents and valuables. Work as fast as you can. Go! Go! Go!"

All six boys scrambled to their duties, crawling over the scene of devastation like rats at a feast. They grabbed anything that might be of use, tearing guns from lifeless hands, whipping watches from shattered wrists, and snatching wallets, passports and jewellery. They stuffed the loot into worn canvas bags before running to the next task. Papers and documents, fluttering on the road like injured birds, were seized and stashed inside shirts. Unexploded mines were dug up and disarmed. The mounted machine gun was expertly stripped down, its heavy carcass left behind.

The boys had to move fast, fast, fast. There was no telling how long they had before they were discovered. At any moment, local tribesmen on their way to the valley fields could appear round the corner, or a group of scrawny children driving their skinny goats down the mountains, or a crowded bus crammed with villagers clattering and chattering to Poonch market. The hills amplified noise and the boom of the explosions would have carried far. Word of the ambush might already have reached the town, and police might be gathering in the main square, ready to investigate.

Nothing stayed secret for long in these mountains.

In minutes the boys' scavenging was done and they fled the scene, clambering over rocks and up steep trails, hauling their plunder, melting quickly into the fabric of the dry brown hills from which they had come. The only evidence that they had been there at all was the discarded carnage they left behind them.

1

Five years earlier

"Jameela! Go and find your brothers. Food's ready and your father wants them here."

Her mother's voice had an edge of impatience to it. She was squatting next to the cooking stove beneath the shade of the walnut tree, grinding spices and patting out chapattis. The meal was prepared, her husband was home from his day's work in the bicycle shop, yet her older sons were nowhere to be seen. Seven-year-old Jameela immediately tossed away the small heap of stones and twigs with which she had been amusing her little sister, Afrah, and jumped up, taking the toddler by the hand.

"Come on, Afrah. Let's go and find Rafiq so Papa's not waiting."

"Take Imraan also," her mother said, indicating the infant gurgling on the mat beside her.

Jameela scooped up the baby, propping him on her hip,

and the little trio headed out of their small courtyard and down the dirt track to the square in front of the mosque.

"We'll look in the square first," she told Afrah. "That's where they always go after school."

Sure enough, there was Rafiq, racing around with his friends, dodging behind the plum trees and swinging from the lower branches. Spits of dust kicked up from his bare heels as he ran. On the wall at one side of the square stood little Mahmood, jumping up and down and waving his arms above his head. "Run, Rafiq, run! They'll catch you. Quick! Quick!" He didn't even see Jameela approach.

"Mahmood, you're to come home now. Dinner's ready."

He turned to her, a scowl darkening his small face. "What about Rafiq? Does he have to come too?"

Mahmood only did what his big brother did, copying him at everything.

Jameela tugged his arm. "You both have to come. Mamma said to get you."

He pulled away from her and clambered down from the wall so she couldn't reach him. "Then call him. I'll wait."

He stood crossly with his arms folded, turned slightly away from her. Jameela knew Rafiq wouldn't want to come home. He might be angry.

"You call him," she suggested to Mahmood archly. "I can't run after him with Afrah and Imraan. And girls don't run after their big brothers. But you can. Show me how quickly you can catch him."

Mahmood was delighted to have an excuse to race

after Rafiq and needed no further encouragement. He forgot about being annoyed and sprinted across the square to where the older boys were now playing.

"Rafiq! Rafiq!" he shouted.

Rafiq stopped his play and stood talking to Mahmood for a moment. He looked over and, after a pause, took leave of his friends and crossed the square. He was hot from running, his face flushed. As Jameela expected, he was not pleased at having to stop. And he certainly did not like being summoned home by his sister.

"Why do we have to go home?" he demanded once Jameela was within earshot.

"Papa's waiting," she told him. "You have to come."

"Mahmood said Mamma sent you."

Jameela grinned. "But it is Papa who wants you."

He knew there was no answer to that. Their father's word was final. Rafiq went in search of his cloth slippers, heaped with the other boys' under one of the plum trees, and slipped them on. They turned up the street and made for home.

"I can run faster than all the boys in my class," Rafiq told Jameela, dancing along beside her. "That's because I'm the tallest."

Jameela kept walking.

"And I'm the best writer also." And when she didn't respond: "Did you hear me?"

"Yes. But I already know," she said, glancing at him. "You don't need to tell me."

"How do you know?" he asked, suddenly curious.

"Because when you teach me from your books, I see the teacher's marks and there are always stars beside your work."

Now it was Rafiq's turn to grin. "You're smart," he said, "for a girl."

Jameela longed to go to school, but in her village, girls didn't attend lessons. Instead they stayed at home and helped their mothers with cooking and cleaning and household tasks. Only the boys went to school, where they learned prayers and writing and reading. Rafiq was clever in school, but once it was over for the day, he threw his books aside to run and play football with his friends in the square.

That evening, when the meal was over and all the village boys were in their homes for the night, the family sat in the courtyard. Rafiq pulled out his books to teach Jameela, as he did most evenings.

"You're wasting your time, Rafiq," their father said as he came out of the house, picking his teeth with the tip of his long knife. "What use has a girl for reading and writing?"

"Teacher says to learn something new every day, Papa," Rafiq dared to answer. "Jameela's learning to read. She's clever. She knows her numbers already."

Jameela smiled up at her father, but he spat against the wall the red juice from the betel nut he was chewing.

"And she'll forget them quickly enough when she is married and she is busy preparing food, taking care of her husband and giving him children. Those are the skills she needs to learn."

"I can write my name, Papa," Jameela piped up.

He looked down at her. "Just make sure you've done your chores first, and Rafiq, your homework."

Rafiq dropped his eyes immediately, in deference to their father's final word, but he wished he would say good things about Jameela's reading and writing. It was true that she didn't need to learn schoolwork, but she enjoyed it and Rafiq liked teaching her, sitting close on the step and reading out the words so she could repeat them. Rafiq thought that sometime, if he felt very brave, he might try to explain this to his papa, even though he knew it would anger him.

As their father left the courtyard to meet with the other men before evening prayers, he glanced to where the golden sun was dipping towards the distant hills. "Rafiq, meet me at the mosque before the sun settles in the Haji Pir pass."

Once her husband had gone, the children's mother spoke up. "It's useful to be able to read and write, Jameela," she said. "Then the traders won't try to cheat you with their prices at market."

Until now she had remained silent, squatting on a mat spread in the corner, where she was busy stitching pieces of brightly coloured cloth into new clothes for her children. She squinted into the last beams of the evening sun to thread the needle she held tightly in one hand.

Jameela smiled at her. "I'll keep learning, Mamma." She looked at Rafiq. "As long as you keep teaching me."

"I like teaching," Rafiq said, his solemn thoughts brightening. "I'd like to be a teacher some day. I'll have girls in my class too, not just boys."

"Can I be in your class, Rafiq?" Mahmood asked, jumping up from where he was drawing in the dust with a small stick. He leaned on his brother's knee.

"You'll be too old to be my pupil," Rafiq told him. "But in less than one year from now, little brother, you'll start school and we can go together."

"And me," cried Afrah, toddling over to join in the chatter.

"Afrah, Afrah!" Rafiq picked her up, laughing, and swung her in the air so she squealed with excitement. "Yes! I'll have you in my class. But not Jameela."

"Why can she be in your class and I can't?" Jameela demanded playfully. Her hands were on her hips, her head cocked to one side, and her mother smiled to see her own mannerisms echoed in her daughter's movements.

Rafiq arched an eyebrow. "Because you'll be married and living far away with your husband."

"I will not!" Jameela spluttered. "I'm not leaving here" – she swept her hand around the courtyard – "to go and get married. I'm staying."

"Ah, you'll change, Jameela. Wait and see," he teased her.

"No, I won't. I will never go away from you, Rafiq,"

she told him, her face suddenly earnest.

Rafiq swung Afrah back to the ground and picked up the books that had been knocked off the step. He blew the dust of the courtyard off them and looked at Jameela. "Then we'll stay together. You'll never get married—"

"And *you'll* never get married," Jameela finished off, laughing.

Their mother gathered up her rolls of cloth and folded the half-finished garments. The light had dimmed and it was too difficult to see the silky threads on the richly patterned fabrics. She carefully wound her spools and packed them with the brass thimble and needles into her wooden sewing box.

"There's no point the two of you discussing matters over which you have no control," she told her two oldest children as she leaned over to check on baby Imraan, who was sleeping peacefully in a sling tied to the lower branches of the walnut tree. Then she stood stiffly to go into the small house, stretching her back as she straightened up. "None of us know how things may change in the coming years."

2

The men came early the next morning.

School was just starting. The air was still cool and the dawn light hazy. The first boys to arrive had sleepily pushed back the sliding doors of the classrooms, opening them up to the schoolyard. The children gathered in the open air, Rafiq among them, drowsy and daydreaming. Even the teachers didn't look awake yet. The boys were standing in line, reciting their early morning prayers, when they heard shouting and the sound of a heavy engine roaring down the street.

"Keep at your prayers, boys. Nothing should come between you and your time with Allah," the headmaster told them. He walked among the rows of children, prodding a fidgety child here, pushing down a lifted head there.

Although the cadence of familiar prayers continued smoothly, everyone was now cocking an ear to the commotion in the village. As soon as the shadow of the headmaster passed where he stood, Rafiq opened his eyes and peeked round. To his disappointment, there was nothing to see. The school gate stood open but the street outside was empty. It was all happening further down the village.

A shot from a gun made them all jump with fright, even the headmaster. Prayer time was abandoned as boys scattered, shouting and running around the schoolyard in panic.

"Quick! Quick! Into the school," the headmaster called out. He grabbed some of the younger children by the scruff of the neck and shoved them towards the open classrooms.

One of the teachers raced across to shut and lock the school gate, while the others called after frightened boys, pulling them into the building. "Quickly, in here. Get out of the yard."

Once inside the classrooms, they dived under their desks, pushing and shoving to find a space to hide. The desks clattered and crashed; the children chattered and babbled, crouching tightly together, some of them giggling nervously.

"Stay still, boys," the teachers told them. "Keep your heads down. Shh! No talking." But it was hard to keep them quiet.

"I think they're close by!"

"Can you hear a truck? It's a big one."

"I hear gunfire. It's very near."

"Sir, they sound like they're outside the school!"

"What will we do?"

More explosions, closer than the first, silenced them all suddenly. The shooting and shouting were getting nearer. For a few seconds, there was quiet, then more shots came, loud and cracking. They split the air and made the boys' ears ring. Sometimes they were single volleys, other times loud bursts of machine-gun fire. The ragged, irregular intervals between the gunfire made it difficult to identify its direction, to anticipate it. It seemed to be right inside the school, in the classrooms, in their heads.

Rafiq jumped with each outburst, his heart pounding as he crouched low and gripped the legs of the desk. He looked out of the open doors to the yard, where suddenly a peppering of bullets pulverized the blue plaster of the school wall. He watched, fascinated, as the dry mortar exploded outwards.

There was a crash as the gate burst open, its lock smashing apart and flying into the air.

Then the men with the guns appeared.

In the schoolyard.

Right outside the classrooms.

In front of the frightened children and their crouching teachers.

The first man sprinted in, his gun slung low on his hip, watched in astonished silence by the schoolboys from under their wooden desks. He was followed by four more men, all wearing orange bandannas tied across their faces so that only their black eyes showed under heavy brows.

They didn't look at the boys at all. Instead they turned and fired their guns back into the street, bullets flashing from the barrels. The noise was so deafening that Rafiq thought his eardrums would burst. The littlest boys howled for their mammas and wet their trousers with fright. The teachers threw their hands up in terror and prayed for deliverance. Rafiq covered his ears and squeezed his eyes shut.

Then the gunfire stopped and there was complete silence. Rafiq felt the hairs on the back of his neck rise and prickle and he knew something bad was happening. Slowly he opened his eyes to see three masked men standing in the classroom.

In the classroom! Rafiq's stomach lurched and his hands trembled as he stared at the heavy boots and trouser legs right in front of where he hid. The men grabbed the desks from above the boys' heads and hurled them into the yard, where they crashed to the ground and splintered. The boys and their teachers were left, exposed, cowering on the empty floor. They scuttled and shuffled together, seeking protection by clustering in a tight knot. But there was nowhere to hide.

"Get out! Move! Into the yard! Now!"

The men grabbed the boys by their hair, by their arms, by their ankles, and yanked and hauled them outside. Children screamed as they were dragged, bumping down concrete steps, knocking against door frames, tripping and falling over one another until they stood, confused and frightened, in the schoolyard. The teachers too were jabbed and shoved, threatened and bullied, until they stood submissively behind the boys, their heads down, their hands clasped low on their stomachs.

The men swung the gate shut and one stood guarding it. The others surrounded the group, waving their guns around wildly and pointing them at the howling boys.

"Do you want to get shot? Do you want to die?" they shouted in their ears, their foul breath hot in the faces of the boys. "We will kill you now. We don't care about your worthless lives."

"Please, sirs, do not harm any of the children." It was the headmaster. He stepped forward and appealed to the men, lifting his hands. "They are good boys. They are only young. Please—"

A rifle butt smashed in his face cut off his words. He collapsed on the ground, calling for help, but the teachers and boys were too frightened to move as he slumped down, blood soaking into the earth from a gash above his eye.

"Now you know what happens if you don't obey us," the men shouted.

One of them went into the nearest classroom and stepped up to the blackboard.

"We are going to have a lesson," he said.

The other men laughed and spat red betel nut juice on the dirt, grinding it in with their boots. Once their laughter died down, there was silence as the man at the board took up a piece of chalk and drew a line along the wall of the classroom. Rafiq heard the dry scraping on the plaster and saw the chalk dust drifting in the air.

"Now we do some measuring. Every boy must come up to this line and stand against it. If you are smaller than the line, you go home to your family. If you are taller than the line, you come with us in our big truck for a drive into the mountains. Get in line!"

The boys shuffled into a ragged queue aided by prods and pokes from the gunmen's rifles. Rafiq joined it, but his heart was low. He knew well before he got to it that he was taller than that line. Never in his life had he so regretted being tall for his age. Usually he was proud of it. Standing a good head above his friends was a great advantage when they played football, because Rafiq always got chosen. But now, height was a bad thing.

The queue of boys in front of Rafiq moved forward quickly. The little six- and seven-year-olds weren't even measured. They were herded together under the care of the teachers and the watch of one of the gunmen. It was the turn of Rafiq's friends: the eight- and nine-year-olds. As they moved into the classroom, he smelt chalk dust mingled with the odour of fear and the sweat of the militants.

One by one the children stepped forward and stood against the chalk line. The head of every nine-year-old in the school grazed the bottom of the mark and they were dismissed to the yard. They ran into the sunshine, smiling with relief. They were free.

Rafiq's turn came and he stepped up to the chalk line. It reached the top of his ear.

"This one is big enough."

The man who stood beside Rafiq dropped a dirty hand on his small shoulder and spoke to the others.

"He goes in the truck. He's our first."

Rafiq looked out at his friends clustered in the bright sunshine. They stood staring in at him, their eyes wide. The heavy hand on his shoulder jerked him away to the dark side of the classroom. He was the first to be selected from his whole school. The first boy to measure over the line. The youngest boy to be chosen. He stood to one side, feeling numb and bewildered.

Gradually more boys joined him and they stood awkwardly, shuffling and silent, until the gunmen had completed their task. Three of the men surrounded the group of small children and teachers and lifted their guns. The teachers cried for mercy; the boys whimpered. The chosen boys stared in shock. One of the men turned to Rafiq and his group.

"We are leaving now. You are coming with us," he said, his voice hard as stone. "Get into the truck calmly and in silence. Any noise or escape attempts and every child and teacher here will be shot dead. It is up to you to keep them alive. Understand?"

The street outside the school was quiet and empty. The gunshots had cleared the usual collection of hawkers and stallholders from their perches. The egg seller had scooped in her fragile collection of hen and goose eggs. The old man who fried onion bhajis had disappeared. The only signs of life were a cow chewing a cardboard box and a couple of dogs sniffing a vat of cooking oil still bubbling over its furnace. No one was there to see more than half of the boys from the village school scramble, sobbing, into the back of the truck.

Once they were in, the gunmen slammed shut the heavy door and slid the metal bolt into place. The terrified boys crouched in darkness and silence. Rafiq heard the men clamber onto the tarpaulin roof. The cab door slammed and the engine guttered into life. With a lurch they roared away from the village.

3

They travelled for many hours in the back of the truck, falling against one another and pitching around as it bumped over dirt tracks. The heat was unbearable, and the boys grew sleepy and listless from lack of air. Several of them peed where they squatted and the floor fouled up. Rafiq's shirt was damp with sweat. He hunkered in a corner and stared into the darkness, wondering where he was going and what was happening. He knew he'd get into trouble for being late home, and hoped the men with guns would bring him back soon because Jameela would never find him if she went looking. With a flush of shame he thought of his father, who would be angry if Rafiq was late for evening prayers. But there was nothing he could do.

When they finally stopped, the men climbed off the roof and opened the back door. "Get out!" they shouted, grabbing the boys nearest the door. "Over here! Quickly! In line!"

The boys clambered out, stumbling with confusion. Rafiq squinted in the bright light, although the white heat of the day had passed. The sun had risen and dropped again, and he realized with dismay that the time he was expected to be home for his meal had come and gone.

When the dry dust raised by the wheels had settled, they stared around them, salty sweat dripping from their hair and stinging their eyes. The flat desert plains that surrounded their village fields had vanished. Now they were encircled by rolling brown hills. Rafiq looked at them and knew with a sinking heart that he was a very long way from home. He guessed they had travelled north. Last year he had gone north with his father to the town of Varahamula and these hills looked the same, but he wasn't certain.

The truck had stopped beneath a scattering of leafless trees, and when Rafiq gazed up at their black shrivelled branches, he thought they looked like giant spider legs, stretching creepily for the sky. He shuddered and turned away to see that his captors had removed their orange bandannas, showing dark faces with greasy beards. One of them produced a large cooking pot, which he put on the ground beneath the shade of a spider-leg tree.

"Eat some food or you'll be too weak for the journey," he told them.

The boys were ravenous. They clustered around the pot, peering hungrily at the cold rice. Another gunman appeared carrying a second pot full of dhal. Rafiq's mouth watered. It was a long time since he'd had chapattis and tea before school that morning. One of the gunmen scooped a ladle of rice onto a banana leaf, dolloped some dhal on top, then held it out. There was a skirmish as boys grabbed and jumped and reached for the food, dirty hands pushing and shoving, spilling rice and dhal on the ground. A tall boy with a cut lip managed to snatch it with both hands. He elbowed others out of the way and scampered off, stuffing handfuls of food into his mouth, dhal and rice dribbling down his chin. The scuffling around the pot continued, with the older, stronger boys getting their food first, leaving the smaller boys to squabble over the diminishing mound of rice.

Rafiq was one of the last to be fed and worried there'd be no food for him. The tin ladle was scraping the bottom of the pot by the time he got close. Some of the older boys had already finished their rice by then and were beginning to skulk around the pot again like hungry dogs. Rafiq watched them warily, poking his elbows out to fend off their advances. He wasn't about to go hungry. As soon as he managed to get his hands on a banana leaf of rice and dhal, he spat on top to protect it, then scurried away to gobble it down.

One of the gunmen put out a wooden bowl of drinking water and a ladle and let the boys help themselves, resulting in more squabbling and fighting.

"Now you can have a break," he told them. "See!

We are not cruel men. We are taking care of you – feeding you and giving you water to drink." The other men laughed. "Now we are letting you rest in the shade."

The boys squatted in silence, drinking in the fresh air, afraid to speak. Their captors hunkered around the perimeter, eating their own meal, their guns cocked. They seemed more relaxed now they were away from the village and joked among themselves and smoked cigarettes. One of them tended to the truck, which looked old and belched steam from beneath the bonnet.

Rafiq watched them, the sharp fear he had felt earlier in his stomach replaced with a sick feeling that wouldn't go away. He wanted to be at home, to be away from these dangerous strangers and this empty place, but was afraid to move. He was torn between doing what he was told and wanting to flee across the desert. He wondered if he would get far, and if they'd beat him if they caught him.

His father had taught him that it was disrespectful to disobey adults, because there was much to learn from them: they knew more than children. Rafiq looked at the men who had dragged him from his classroom and dumped him in the back of a reeking truck for hours, and doubted that these were the kind of adults his father had meant. He studied them carefully. They looked dirty and dangerous, chewing and belching as they squatted on the ground with their guns all around them. He wondered what there was to learn from them. It didn't look like they knew more than he did about anything much, except maybe when Rafiq and the other boys would be taken home.

A couple of older boys started to mutter to each other. Rafiq listened to their conversation.

"We should demand to be returned to our families," one whispered softly. "We have done nothing wrong." He glanced at the gunmen as he spoke, but it didn't sound like he was going to do any demanding.

"They've no right to kidnap us," the other boy agreed. "We should tell them how we feel."

But neither of them moved towards the gunmen. After all, they had witnessed what had happened to the headmaster. They weren't that foolish.

Two boys next to Rafiq were crying, sobbing miserably, their arms round each other. "We're going to die," they spluttered. "We'll never see our families again and we'll be killed."

They turned to Rafiq, seeking to bring him into their group, but he looked away from them. He could understand how they felt, but they shouldn't cry. It wasn't honourable behaviour and they were shaming their families by weeping in the dirt like little girls, by showing their emotions so openly. Had they no pride?

Once, when Rafiq had been a small boy, he had become separated from his family when tribal traders passed through his village. The whole square was filled with camels and goats. The strangers rolled woven rugs out on the ground and sold jewellery and bolts of cloth, dried spices and electronic goods. Rafiq had been mesmerized, wandering from trader to trader with his parents. One minute, he was beside his mother; the next, he looked up and she had gone, vanished into the heaving masses of people who laughed and shouted and struck deals.

Rafiq looked around in panic, but couldn't see her skirts anywhere. He called her again and again, but she didn't answer. He was surrounded by a forest of legs as tall strangers traded and carried on with their business way above his small head. They ignored the upset child who squeezed, panicked, through the seething crowds. Rafiq's fear filled his head and sickened his stomach. What if he couldn't find his mamma? What if she had left him? The legs surrounding him pressed closer and closer. He was locked in. He pushed against them but they were solid and unyielding. His face got hot and flushed. Finally he opened his mouth and howled, his whole body so full of terror that it spilled out of him in a huge wave of sobbing and screaming. That got everyone's attention.

Suddenly there was space around him as people pulled back to look at the small being who was making such a huge commotion. Bartering and arguing ceased as everyone near by stopped to listen. Children peeked out from behind their parents' legs, pressing their hands over their ears. Rafiq continued to scream, feeling even more frightened now that everyone was staring at him.

Then, out of the crowds, his father appeared. He scooped Rafiq up, swung him onto his shoulders and strode through the watching crowds. The space melted away to nothing. Rafiq stopped screaming. He could see the bobbing heads below him and was safe in his father's arms, although for a long time afterwards his small body was racked with sobs. In the distance he could see his relieved mother waving at him, baby Jameela on her hip.

Later that night, his father talked gently to him, holding his small son on his lap. The kerosene lamp on the floor guttered and smoked, throwing shadows across his face.

"When you are not with your family, Rafiq, you must be strong. You must not show your feelings for the whole world to see, for that brings shame on your mother and father. These emotions are private, and should be kept private. On the outside you must be calm and brave, even if inside you are not feeling calm and brave. You must always be proud and courageous and bring honour to your people."

Rafiq felt his face flush when he realized he had brought shame on his family by his behaviour in the square. It was a lesson he would never forget. He would never shame his family again.

The light and heat softened further and the brown hills darkened. When the sun was lower in the sky, the men stood up. They stretched and farted, spat betel juice and angled their guns at the children.

"Enough rest. Into the truck again. All of you. We still have far to go."

The boys shambled reluctantly towards the stinking truck. All except one.

"I don't want to go in there," this boy protested shrilly, pulling back, bumping against the others.

"Get in!" ordered one of the men and grabbed his shoulder, but the boy twisted sharply away.

"Leave me alone," he cried. "I want to go home to my family."

Another captor caught him by the shirt and was about to lift him bodily into the vehicle, when the boy suddenly ducked and ran. He zigzagged wildly across the desert, his heels kicking up spits of dust. The gunman yelled at the others and fired into the air, causing panic and confusion among the children. They screamed and cowered, several of them running off in blind terror, but the men seized the panicked boys and flung them into the truck. They pointed their rifles at the petrified children.

"Stay there or we kill you!"

The escaped boy was still racing, moving in an arc to the left. Two men sprinted after the runaway, shouting at him and shooting into the air. But he had the edge on them and moved fast, his skinny legs pelting along. The men stopped the chase. Muzzles flashed as bullets exploded out. Gunfire filled the air and blue smoke drifted upwards.

The rest of the boys huddled in shocked silence in the back of the truck. When the smoke cleared, the boy was no longer running. They all stared. In the distance they could see his body crumpled in the dirt. The door of the truck was slammed shut and they drove off into the vast expanse of the dusty hills.

And in the dark, airless interior Rafiq felt his heart hammer against his chest as he thought how he might have been that boy sprinting into the desert, trying to escape.

4

In the village the roar of the truck had faded swiftly into the distance. Other sounds rose in the schoolyard to break the aching emptiness. They were pale, feathery sounds that hurt the air. Small boys sobbed uncontrollably, whimpering and snivelling. They crowded together, not knowing what to do but feeling safer in a tight huddled knot. The headmaster moaned softly as he struggled to his feet, blood seeping from his wound.

At first the teachers whispered timidly. Raising their voices to speak seemed too forceful, too shocking, after the terrible events. They fussed around the headmaster, righting a chair so he could sit down, washing out a piece of cloth to hold against the wound. But they moved slowly as though their limbs were filled with sand. Even the boys, who normally dipped and dashed like swallows after a fly, appeared to have no energy. Fast movements jarred their raw senses. There had been distress enough for one day.

"Do you think they've gone?" asked one of the teachers quietly, voicing everyone's question. They all looked at him but nobody answered. He picked a boy with round frightened eyes. "Go and find out," he directed, giving him a nudge on the shoulder. "Don't be seen by anyone. Just have a quick look."

They stayed clustered together as the trembling child crept along the shadow of the wall to the smashed gate and cautiously stuck out his head. Quicker than a gasp he turned and raced back, his face wild, his skinny arms held stiffly by his sides.

"Everyone's gone," he reported frantically, his eyes stretched and circled with white. "They've taken everyone from the village. The street's empty. No one's left. Only us."

And immediately he started to howl, setting off the other children until their wails shattered the fragile security that had begun to gather. Amidst their terrible keening the headmaster rose wearily to his feet and stumbled unsteadily towards the gate. When the teachers realized where he was going, they hung back sheepishly, wringing their hands and shaking their heads. Two boys offered their small hands to the headmaster instead; he glanced down and grasped them tightly. Together they walked slowly towards the street. The teachers waited, their arms wrapped protectively round their bodies, their faces paralysed with fear.

The headmaster passed through the gateway and disappeared. The teachers looked at each other. The children looked to their teachers, but saw only confusion and uncertainty. One by one the boys turned towards the empty gate. They weren't about to be left behind. Their legs found the energy they needed and they took off, racing out of the schoolyard, out of the gate, and pounding down the empty street, overtaking the shaken headmaster and his two small companions.

Their thumping feet brought cautious peeks from the villagers still hiding in their dark houses and in the back rooms of their shops. They squinted out warily, not certain if the noise came from the militants, and were astonished to see the smallest boys from the school pouring through the streets, pelting wildly towards their homes. And, following behind, the stumbling beaten-up headmaster, with his bloody eye and improvised bandage.

The sight drew gasps of shock from the staring villagers, who ran out onto the street to offer assistance. A chair. A drink of water. A clean cloth. But the headmaster waved away offers of help. He kept walking slowly, his good eye staring resolutely ahead, his grip on the two boys firm. And some dark insight drew the villagers along with him, a terrible coldness crawling beneath their skin. Its blackness seeped into their bones, lurking deep in the marrow, as they sensed that this was a day like no other.

A day they would talk about for ever.

When the headmaster reached the square, he freed the

two boys and slumped on the perimeter wall. It was as if he had drawn strength from them, and now that they were released he had no power of his own. The crowd swelled in number as people flocked to the square on hearing that something dreadful had happened. Men came rushing from their work, abandoning stalls, deserting looms, animals and fields. Women ran from their homes, carrying infants, forgetting bubbling pots and sizzling pans, leaving water jars half filled. Older girls arrived, dragging little brothers and sisters by the hands, hurrying through the streets of the village. The people jostled and pushed, stretched their necks and whispered to one another, while the headmaster sat silently, staring at the ground.

Finally he spoke, and they listened in stunned silence as he told them what had happened.

Jameela bobbed with Mahmood and Afrah at the fringes of the crowd, straining to hear what was being said. The headmaster's cracked voice didn't carry far and the ears of those at the front quickly swallowed his words, so she caught only fragments. She tugged at the sleeve of the woman in front of her.

"What is it?" she asked. "What's he saying?"

The woman turned, her scarf pulled closely around her face, her eyes wet with tears.

"The boys. They've taken the boys. All the big boys have been taken from the school."

"Who? Who's taken them?" Jameela wanted to know, but the woman had turned back to hear more.

Flickers of lament began to curl from the heart of the crowd. They were slender and reedy at first, just a few threads twisting upwards, some lone voices. But they quickly multiplied, drawing on the grief and despair gathered in one place, sucking on the souls of everybody who stood around the crippled headmaster. The cries became louder and thicker, building into an alarming crescendo. Jameela was frightened. She wanted to find her mother and Imraan. They had come to the square with them but were lost among the nudging, pressing people. Afrah and Mahmood started crying, disturbed by the loud keening and dark mood of the people.

Jameela tried to comfort them. "We'll find Mamma. Everything will be fine."

But they were howling now, their faces flushed. Jameela skirted the edge of the seething crowd, searching for the familiar colours of her mother's shawl, for Imraan's little face. The mothers' weeping rose and fell in a haunting lilt that thickened the air with sadness. It was chilling to hear.

Everyone around Jameela was talking at once, crying and shouting. The other teachers had arrived and people clustered around them, demanding answers, trying to understand the appalling thing that had happened. The fathers began to group together to one side. They thumped their fists into the palms of their hands and punched the air with fury. Jameela could see her papa in the midst of them, but he wasn't shouting or thumping his fists. Instead he was standing still, his eyes gazing into some far distance but seeing nothing. Jameela stopped momentarily, taken aback by the sorrow etched into his face. Her heart ached for him. She longed to go to him but could not. She moved away from the men and found where the women had clustered together with the children and babies.

"There's Mamma," Afrah cried.

They pushed their way through the other children to clutch at her skirts. She turned, and in one movement crouched down and gathered all her precious children into her arms. All except one.

"What's happened?" Jameela asked, looking at her mother's tear-stained face.

"They've taken Rafiq," she whispered. "My first child. My eldest son." She shook her head, not believing her own words. "All the boys over ten have been taken. Men with guns snatched them all." Her face crumpled and she wept, still holding on to her other children.

Jameela felt her head spin. Rafiq. Her older brother. Taken from school by bad men. But she thought of something: Rafiq was only nine, not ten until his next birthday.

"Mamma," she said. "He's not ten. They wouldn't have taken him. He's only nine. They must have left him behind."

Her mother lifted her head and looked at her young daughter, fixing a loose strand of hair behind Jameela's ear.

"But he's tall. They thought he was older. All his friends were left behind, but Rafiq is tall and strong and they took him, even though he is only nine years old. His teacher said he was the first to be chosen."

She couldn't say any more as her body was convulsed by shuddering sobs. It broke Jameela's heart but all she could do was stand beside her mother, stroking her bent head, tears streaming down her own face. The shouting of the men faded and Jameela looked up to see them leaving the square as one group.

"Where are they going?"

"Perhaps to follow? Let's go and see," replied her mother.

They were not the only family to trail after the men. Little by little the square emptied. Some of the fathers disappeared into their homes and shops, emerging moments later carrying makeshift weapons: digging forks and spades, butchers' knives and cooking implements. Anything they could lay their hands on. Anything that might be of use.

They gathered outside the school, waiting. The women and children clustered to one side, watching. There was much talk about directions and routes, with a great deal of animated gesturing and frantic pointing. The schoolteachers were there too, although Jameela didn't think they looked as eager as the other men. They stood together, looking around them fretfully. It had been decided that the headmaster should stay behind. He had been through enough.

She could see her father standing quietly, resolutely, his hand resting on the shaft of his old rake, and she prayed that he would be safe, that he would bring Rafiq home. Some women handed over bundles of food: oven-warm bread, hard-boiled eggs, dried meat. The men were anxious about how late it was already, how far the militants' truck might have travelled. With every second breath, they impatiently looked up and down the streets of the village.

Finally, with a clamour and a cloud of dust, those in the village who owned vehicles arrived. The few cars and vans, and even four scooters, stopped haphazardly and the men piled in, cramming into every available space, fitting in an astonishing number of bodies. And then they were off, roaring down the road in pursuit of the truck that had carried away their sons.

It was a long day for those left behind. The boys had been taken at dawn; now the streets were hot and the sun was high in the sky. The women and children stood in confusion, unable to return to their daily tasks. They found themselves drawn to the school in an effort to warm their hearts on the lingering spirits of the boys, to understand in some way what had happened. They saw the smashed gate and the scattered broken furniture. They stared in silence at the bloodstain in the dust. They stood mutely in one classroom, gazing at a roughly drawn chalk line on the wall; at chalk crushed into the floor.

It was after dark when the men returned. The women and children heard the engines and saw the lights in the distance. By the time the vehicles pulled up outside the school, there was a crowd waiting for them. The men climbed out of the cramped spaces with drained faces and stiff limbs. They were alone. They stood in awkward silence, gazing bleakly at the ground. They carried their weapons slackly. None of them had been used.

"They have vanished," one man stated. "We drove for nine hours. We searched everywhere. We found nothing. It is as if they have been swallowed by the mountains."

Jameela glimpsed her father at the back of the group. His face looked sad and empty and she feared he would never recover.

"The police will come from Varahamula," the man continued. "To take statements from everyone. They will not arrive until tomorrow afternoon. After that…"

His voice trailed away forlornly. Because nobody knew.

Back at their home Jameela's mother lit the stove and began to prepare food like she always did, except that tears kept dripping from her face and sizzling in the hot pan. Mahmood sat in the dirt, lost about what to do now that Rafiq wasn't coming home. The baby sucked his fist and rocked in the hammock while Afrah stood holding Jameela's hand, gazing up at her, her brown eyes round and frightened. Jameela waited for a while, looking to her mother, but there was no discussion, no change in routine.

"Go and put the little ones to bed," her mother told her.

And so she did.

5

The truck thundered along rutted roads, throwing the boys from side to side. When it climbed steep tracks, the gears whined and protested. When the potholes were deep, the tyres spun uselessly in the dry dirt. It seemed like they were driving to the end of the earth. Finally they slowed and stopped. The engine was switched off. The gunmen climbed off the tarpaulin roof and slid the bolt from the door. It crashed open.

Rafiq blinked and lifted his head. It was night-time and the air that poured in was fresh and hushed, full of the smell of vegetation. The dustiness of the desert had been replaced by a warm dampness. The children clambered out of the stinking vehicle and stood, stupid with tiredness and confusion. Rafiq hoped he could rest soon. His legs and arms ached and his head was throbbing. How much longer would this day last?

"Into line – one behind the other."

The voices of the gunmen were less frightening now, but Rafiq didn't know if that was because he was getting used to them, or because it was late and they were also tired. There was rough pushing, shoving. Many of the boys cried out and sobbed, but Rafiq was silent. Instead he watched. He wanted to learn about the men. He knew they were ruthless and didn't care about the boys. But when were they not paying attention? When were they careless? Rafiq wanted to watch for chances to get away. Would an opportunity come for him? The men squatted down and moved along the line of grubby boys. Dirty hands fumbled with heavy rope, tying it tightly around the ankles of each child so they were linked together. The boy at the front of the line was given a shove.

"Walk!"

The children stumbled through undergrowth, struggling as the rope scuffed and scraped at their ankles. They groped their way through dense shrubbery where vines and tree roots tripped them. The men spread along the length of the line, jostling the children, butting them with the barrels of their guns.

"No slowing down. Walk quicker!"

"Keep up the pace. You're holding us up."

Eventually they arrived at a waterhole, its muddy banks gleaming in the moonlight.

"Drink here," the leading gunman told them.

Rafiq and the other children sank to their knees and

drank thirstily. A small herd of goats watched from the far side of the pool, their bells clanging softly. Rafiq sat back on his ankles and thought of the goats at home. Who would milk them tonight, he wondered – and would Jameela remember to slide the bolt on the shed to keep the foxes from the chickens and the new kid? If not, his father would be furious. In the distance he could see the lights of fires in a settlement and the shadows of huts, but they were not going in that direction. Rafiq squatted miserably and scooped handfuls of dark water to wet his hair and cool his neck.

"Enough. Move."

The gunmen urged them to their feet again and they struggled on. Rafiq had no idea how long they walked. He kept stumbling forward, blindly following the back of the boy in front of him, no longer thinking about where he was going or why. One of his cloth slippers fell off but Rafiq hardly noticed its absence as he trudged on. At last, when the night had folded in on itself, the men called a halt.

"We stay here until dawn," one announced.

Rafiq looked around. There was no village, no water-hole, no bushes. Just a barren hillside with a huge banyan tree spreading its branches.

"And don't bother trying to escape," the man warned. "One of us will be awake – with a gun at the ready."

"Nowhere to go anyway," another gunman mocked as he bent down and released the rope from one ankle of each boy. Several of the boys whimpered as it was wrenched off but Rafiq gritted his teeth and remained quiet. He reached down and massaged his ankle where the rough fibres had cut into his skin, leaving it chafed and bloody. He kicked off his remaining slipper, for it was no use on its own.

One of the gunmen threw rounds of flatbread to the boys. There was the usual grabbing and tussling until each boy got his hands on one to chew. They stuffed them down and looked hungrily for more, but there were none; only water to drink. Then the children clustered against the base of the tree, sheltering among its roots. Some of them slept, but not Rafiq. His eyes darted around rapidly, searching for a gap, an opportunity; but the men had scattered themselves among the boys, their guns ready. One man, who seemed to be the leader, sat above them on a small hillock, watching. The tip of his cigarette glowed red in the dark.

Rafiq lay against the tree and gazed at the sky, feeling the hope that had kept him going seep into the earth. It seemed as though the stars were retreating further away and an endless blackness was reaching for him, soaking up his spirit. His heart beat fast and he was afraid it would shatter into a million fragments that would vanish for ever into the darkness. He wrapped his arms across his chest to stop the trembling and forced himself to look away. Only the previous night, that same sky had blessed him with the light from a million sacred stars. He had been happy then. So happy, he had gone immediately to wake his little sister.

"Jameela! Jameela! Are you asleep?"

She opened her eyes and was instantly awake. Rafiq was kneeling beside her, his eyes large and dark. She propped herself up on her elbow.

"What is it? Is something the matter?"

He smiled at her and shook his head. "Nothing. But I want to show you something. Come on."

He took Jameela's hand and led her outside, across the small courtyard to the hut on the far side. It was a clear night and everything was swimming in a soft silvery light. He knelt down and opened the door of the hut. The hens clucked in alarm at the unexpected intrusion, but Rafiq scattered them with a sweep of his hand. They fluttered out, squawking in protest, and scratched around the yard. He motioned Jameela to kneel down beside him while he reached into the hut.

"I know what it is," Jameela whispered in delight. "The nanny goat has had her kid!"

Rafiq pulled out a newly born kid from a nest of straw. Its coat was still damp and it lay helplessly on the ground.

"I wanted you to be the first to see him," he told Jameela. "I heard the nanny bleating and knew she was going to give birth, so I came down to help her."

The little kid was still wobbly of head and not ready to stand. The nanny goat followed him out of the hut and circled him, fretting and licking his coat. Jameela and Rafiq sat together and watched while she coaxed him to move, gently butting and fussing around him. It took the kid a long time to stand and even then he wobbled on his spindly legs, making the children laugh at his efforts.

Jameela felt sleepy as she rocked gently, gazing at the little kid goat. Rafiq looked at her.

"Come on," he said, smiling. "We'd better go to bed or we'll be late getting up in the morning and Papa will be cross."

He lifted the kid and pushed him back into the hut. His mother followed and they settled on the straw while Rafiq chased the hens back in and shut the door firmly.

"Thank you for showing him to me, Rafiq. He's lovely."

"Tomorrow I'll get a leather strap and a bell to hang around his neck so he won't get lost. Then we'll always know where he is."

They went back into the house, where Jameela checked that Mahmood was asleep, then rolled in beside Afrah, who whimpered.

"Hush, Afrah," Jameela told her, scooping her up and soothing her into her dreams.

Rafiq climbed into his own small cot and lay back. Outside, the stars glittered and the moon cast its cold light across the village. Rafiq settled to sleep, unaware that the next day, his life would change so completely.

6

On the third day, Rafiq climbed with the other boys up, up, up, away from the foothills, driven by their captors. They were moving into the higher hills of the Pir Panjals, where ice crystals sparkled in the shadows and the air was so thin that the children grew breathless. Because they had travelled so far for several days, Rafiq knew that the men must be intending to hold them for some time, but he couldn't imagine where or why. He was so exhausted that he had stopped thinking constantly of when he would get home and trudged on wearily, wondering instead when he could rest. For the first two days, he measured every breath by what he'd normally be doing: walking to school, eating meals, playing football, praying in the mosque. But today was different. There was a different feeling in the air, a different edge to the mood of the gunmen. Today was more significant somehow. Rafiq couldn't work out why, but the change diverted his thoughts from home and made him anxious.

They had started out when the sky was still thick with stars, stumbling blindly upwards over uneven ground. By the time daylight coloured their surroundings, the vegetation had become scrubby and low growing, the trees bony, twisted, wind-bent. The air held on to the night chill, even as the sun climbed above the mountains, and the breeze on their cheeks carried a sharp coldness. The men spoke little among themselves and kept them all moving at a fast pace. There was no food and the only rests were when they stopped to drink at waterfalls spewing icy water from fissures in the rocks.

Rafiq was close to the front of the line when they stopped on a steep slope for the exhausted stragglers at the end to struggle to their feet from where they had collapsed yet again. He stared at the towering teeth of snow-topped peaks and clenched his jaw against the abrasive jerks of the rope.

"Get up! On your feet!" the men were yelling at four boys who lay gasping for air at the end of the line.

Rafiq didn't turn, even when he heard the thumps and whacks as the boys were beaten. He was getting used to it. It didn't even make him tremble any more. A voice close to his ear made him start.

"You are strong for a small boy."

Rafiq flinched and glanced quickly to see one of the gunmen standing close to him. It was the first time any of the men had spoken individually to him, to any of them. Rafiq was too frightened to answer. He stared at the ground instead, not daring to look directly at the man, who continued.

"But I think your spirit is stronger. You will be very useful."

Rafiq saw the man's shadow move away, further down the line, and snatched a fleeting glance after him. He wondered what was meant by his words. Was it good to have a strong spirit? Rafiq wondered if his father would be proud of him for that. He shifted his gaze and looked beyond where the men hauled the broken children to their feet, down the mountainside. In the far distance the immense desert plains spread widely. A broad river meandered across the land, glinting and flashing in the sun. Rafiq squinted his eyes and peered into the distance, but no matter how hard he looked, he couldn't see his village.

They struggled onwards to arid rocky highlands, sometimes crouching on all fours to scramble across seams of black rock and unstable shaley patches that threatened to pitch them into yawning ravines. Rafiq refused to look down at the drops, forcing his trembling legs to hold firm. His hands hunted frantically for finger holds as he clambered across. When he was most afraid, the gunman's words echoed in his head – "You are strong for a small boy" – as if he had seen something in Rafiq that Rafiq himself hadn't known. And it gave him courage to dig deep, to find the strength he needed, knowing his father would be proud of him.

As the day wore on, Rafiq became more and more frustrated with the weak boys at the back. Every time they fell, the slack snapped from the rope, which jerked sharply and bit into Rafiq's raw, bleeding ankles. Every time they fell, he doubled over with pain as the cuts sliced deeper into his flesh. Why couldn't they be strong enough to keep going? They were bigger than he was, but he didn't fall constantly. He felt frustrated and helpless and sore.

Finally he lost his patience. While the gunmen were looking towards the rear of the group, he reached back and grasped a section of the rope, wrenching it upwards with as much force as he could muster, so the stumbling boys would know how it hurt. This caused them to lose their footing completely and to slither, panicked, down the mountainside.

The boys scrabbled frantically, clutching wildly at the surrounding rocks and crying out with terror. The two boys next to Rafiq in the line saw what he had done and their eyes grew wide with disbelief.

"What did you do that for?" one whispered.

"It hurts me every time they fall over," Rafiq tried to explain, blushing as he looked at the stricken boys. "They're bigger than me. They should be stronger."

"They can't help it," the other boy muttered, turning away from him.

The men rushed back to the fallen boys and grabbed them by their shirts, hauling them to their feet and cuffing them across the head for being so careless.

And so they continued.

After many hours of struggling, the gunman at the front of the line, the man who had spoken to Rafiq, halted. He waited until they were huddled together on a small ledge that scarcely held them all.

"Untie the rope," he ordered the rest of the guards. "We will take the next part one by one."

Rafiq peered ahead to where a large cluster of boulders clung precariously to the steep slope. He looked down. Hundreds of metres below, dark birds circled on currents of rising air. The wall of the canyon curved away so that its floor was lost some huge distance beneath the belly of the mountain. Wind cleaved through the vast abyss, eddying and whirling, whipping dust and dried leaves into tiny tornadoes. A surge of adrenalin jolted Rafiq's spine, tingling his scalp and fingertips, when he saw the scale of the sheer drop. His heart thumped. The dry air caught his throat as the grimy hands of the gunmen unknotted the rope to release them. He swallowed, but was relieved that he was no longer tied to the others, especially the weak boys at the back. He could trust his own abilities.

"One at a time. Wait till I call you," the lead gunman told them as he strapped his rifle across his chest, freeing his hands. Then he started scrambling over the heap of huge boulders and fallen rocks. In minutes he had scuttled like an insect across the face of the boulders and leaped lightly to the ground on the other side.

"Next," they heard him shouting.

A gunman pointed at Rafiq. "You! Go ahead."

Rafiq stepped onto the first boulder, which rolled beneath his feet. He gasped. He wanted to jump back to the safety of the ledge but the muzzle of a rifle pressing into his back prevented his doing so. Every muscle tensed, and he forced himself to breathe deeply. He studied the rocks. Slowly, carefully, he adjusted his weight, lifting his arms by his sides to find his balance. He began to thread his way nervously, feeling the loose stones rasp and grind beneath his bare feet. Slowly he moved away from the group, edging closer to the far side, placing his feet with care, scanning the boulders for fissures and ledges to cling to. He concentrated hard, sweat trickling between his shoulder blades.

He was spreadeagled on the rocky mound when a sudden gust of wind rose from the floor of the chasm and rushed at him. Rafiq took a gulp of air and flattened himself against the heap of rocks. Behind him he could hear gasps from the watching boys. The wind dropped as abruptly as it had risen, giving him just enough time to lift his body and reach out before it rushed at him a second time, grabbing at his clothing, knocking him off balance. His stretching hand scuffed against roughness, scraping across jagged edges, skinning his knuckles. His fingers scrabbled against the pitted surface, hunting a groove or crevice to hang on to.

Finally he found a narrow fissure above his head. The unsteady rocks underneath him teetered and slipped, grinding against their neighbours. His hand dislodged loose stones and pebbles which cascaded onto him, showering him with grit and sand, before plunging into the abyss. Rafiq gasped with shock, blinded by the blast of sand, as more rocks dislodged and plummeted into the chasm, crashing and pounding through scrub. The watching boys caught their breath and hugged their arms around their shaking bodies. Even the gunmen froze.

Rafiq's knees buckled beneath him as his feet slithered several inches. He clutched at knotted weeds on the eroded boulders, his fingers raking through them. Beneath his feet the stones muttered and complained, settling themselves in their new positions. Rafiq didn't twitch a muscle. He was too terrified to move. Gradually everything stilled again. The breeze dropped to nothing.

"Keep moving," a gunman shouted.

But Rafiq's body was paralysed with shock. He was unable even to lift his head. His knuckles were bone white where they gripped the rock. His eyes were squeezed shut, the muscles in his jaw jumping. The gunman shouted again but Rafiq stayed motionless, his face ashen.

The minutes ticked by. Everyone waited. Eventually a gunman with the boys picked up a stone. He swung his arm. The stone hurtled through the air and cracked against the rock beside Rafiq's face. Rafiq opened his eyes, his pupils huge with terror. He was staring straight down the barrel of the gunman's rifle.

"Move or I shoot," the man told him. "Three. Two…"

Rafiq stared blankly. He blinked and then his eyes

flickered around. Slowly his frozen body stirred. Still gazing down the barrel of the gun, he moved one arm and grabbed hold of a boulder. Gradually he moved away from where he teetered on the edge of the abyss. He groped his way blindly, afraid to lift his eyes from the rock face.

"Turn your head," came the command. "Look where you're going."

Rafiq gripped the rocks with both hands and swivelled to face the direction in which he was crawling, making his torturous way across the remaining gap. When at last he reached the other side, the lead gunman prised him off the boulders and shook him by the shoulders, as if to shake the stiffening fear out of him. Rafiq collapsed on the ground like a loose bag of bones, his limbs slick with sweat, his heart hammering against his ribs.

By the time all the boys were across, it was late afternoon. The gunmen didn't tether them as they moved off and Rafiq sensed a growing anticipation and excitement in their captors as they crested a steep hill. In the distance was a shallow valley sheltered between high hills. There, hidden among brown boulders, Rafiq could see smoke twisting into the air and mud huts clustered in groups. The bright sun flashed on corrugated metal roofs. He made out figures moving among the huts, saw pack mules and horses and heard the clanging of goat bells.

Without warning, the leading gunman lifted his rifle and fired several shots into the air. The boys flinched and ducked their heads as the explosions echoed around the soaring mountains. After a short delay, there was a returning volley of fire from the settlement ahead.

"We're home," the leader announced, spitting betel juice on the ground and grinning broadly.

7

The group straggled down the side of the hill and limped into a flat area in the midst of the huts.

"Sit and don't move," their captors told them.

The boys clustered together nervously and squatted on the ground, looking around. Men appeared from various huts, shouting and calling to the gunmen. They walked over and greetings began: slaps on the back, hugs, laughter. Rafiq listened as the men praised the lead gunman for the successful mission, shouting his name out loud – "Abdullah! Abdullah!" – and firing their guns skywards, which caused the hills to echo. Youths appeared from between the cabins, young boys and teenagers, curious to see what the activity was about. They stared at the new arrivals, who stared back at them. Rafiq hunkered on the ground with the others, not speaking, his muscles aching from the long trek, his mouth parched.

There was a large open fire built next to where the boys waited, walled with mud bricks. Its charcoals glowed chalky white, the heat shimmering the air. The ground around it was packed hard and strewn with splinters of bleached bone and grains of rice at which chickens scratched and rooted. Rafiq glimpsed more huts and fenced areas further away. The settlement was large and scattered.

Beyond the fire was a screened-off section. Through chinks in the woven thatch screens Rafiq caught glimpses of women and children. There was the clang of pots and the dry scrape of pottery: the cooking area. Smoke from cooking stoves drifted upwards, and smells of fresh-baking roti and meat stew drifted out.

A small toddler with a runny nose and a grubby T-shirt tottered out from behind the screens. As Rafiq stared at her, he was reminded of Afrah. The memory was vivid and insistent, to be replaced a second later by another, then another, as Rafiq's thoughts exploded with images of home: Afrah laughing as he tickled her, Jameela handing him lemon tea, Mahmood racing under the plum trees, Imraan perched on his mother's hip. The memories hurt Rafiq's heart and stung his eyes. He wanted more than anything to be with his family, taking care of the goats, playing in the square, but his home seemed a lifetime away.

After a while two women emerged from behind the screens, carrying pots and dishes. They came over to the children and squatted down.

"You must be hungry, boys," the older woman said.

Wordlessly the boys shuffled around her, keeping a wary eye on the gunmen but naturally drawn to her gentleness. Rafiq felt his eyes stinging with sudden tears and he furiously rubbed his hand across his dirty face.

The other woman said nothing, just looked at them from dark eyes, her face hidden by her hijab. She filled an assorted collection of mugs with water, which she handed out. There was none of the usual scuffling and fighting. Each boy waited his turn, then silently took the mug handed to him and drank deeply. They were given bowls of steaming stew with beans, goat meat and rice. The boys accepted what was given to them, muttering thanks, and retreated to devour the food, using their fingers to stuff their mouths full. As they ate, the women went around the group, refilling mugs, handing out rounds of bread, ladling out stew. Rafiq mopped up the juices on his plate, drank more water and belched. His belly was stretched and full of food.

"This is a good home," the man they called Abdullah announced, suddenly appearing next to the boys, his gun resting against his leg.

Rafiq's warm feeling vanished and his muscles stiffened when he heard the voice. He dared not look up at him. Instead he kept his eyes on the ground and hunched his shoulders against any blows. Why does he keep calling this home? Rafiq wondered. This is not my home.

"You will meet many people here. New brothers. New family," Abdullah told them.

Rafiq's gaze lingered on the rough earth at his feet. He had a family. He had sisters and brothers, parents he loved. He wanted to be with them. Not here with these strangers.

"You will learn new things and you will grow to be men."

Rafiq glanced at the other boys who squatted with him. They all had their eyes lowered, their heads tucked between their shoulders. No boy looked happy to be among a new family of unknown men who beat him for no reason.

As the sun fell and the air cooled, Abdullah and another of their new brothers marched the captured boys at gunpoint across a hill and down a rocky slope to a river.

"Clean yourselves," Abdullah ordered. "Wash off everything from your old life that clings to you. You no longer have need of it."

They washed off three days of dirt and sweat and blood. The cold clean water stung their chafed wrists and raw ankles.

By the time they returned to the settlement, the main fire was lit. Its flames were bright and lively, jumping out of the softened light of dusk. The other boys living in the camp placed kerosene lamps around, their yellow light like pools of melted butter on the ground.

"We will pray together," Abdullah told them.

The men stood in front; Rafiq and the other kidnapped boys stood in the centre with the other children; the women stayed separate at the back. Evening prayers began. Rafiq was soothed by the familiar lilt of the imam's voice. He moved through the various positions of kneeling, standing and prostrating.

Afterwards the men remained where they were until the women and little children had gone behind the screens. Then Abdullah turned to the new boys. Randomly separating them, he shoved half towards a small hut adjacent to the central compound.

"Get inside!" he shouted. "The rest of you, over here."

They stumbled after him and were pushed into a second hut on the other side of the fire. The hut was small and cramped. The door slammed behind them and the boys crowded silently in the dark, listening as Abdullah slid across a heavy bolt. As soon as his footsteps receded, Rafiq pressed his eye to a crack in the wall and watched him stride back to the bright fire, where celebrations seemed to be starting. The men sat in large groups, helping themselves to steaming dishes of food served by the women.

Rafiq's breaths came fast and shallow. This was not what he wanted. His face screwed up in disbelief. How was he to get out of this prison? Behind him the boys whispered as they explored the contours of the hut, rolling out sleeping mats, pulling at blankets, squabbling over scraps of floor space.

"They can't leave us here," Rafiq said, his voice splintering at the edges. "I have to go home to my family. They'll be wondering where I am."

There was a sudden hush as the boys listened, but

before Rafiq had even stopped speaking, a dark figure carrying a gun stood up and detached itself from the crowd of men in the central compound. The man strode right up to the door, so close that Rafiq felt the warmth of his breath through the crack. He froze, but kept watching. The man turned and squatted against the door, his rough wool jacket scratching against the wood as he slid to the ground. After a pause the boys resumed their muffled nesting.

Then it occurred to Rafiq that perhaps these men never intended to take him home. Perhaps they wanted him to live with them in their mountain camp, although he couldn't think why. All he could think of was the ache in his bones and the sadness in his heart. And for the first time since the gunmen had appeared in his classroom, tears spilled unchecked down Rafiq's cheeks.

Outside, the guard lifted his rifle and cocked the trigger, the cold sound reaching into the young boy's soul. Rafiq no longer had the strength to stand. He sank to the ground and let the darkness take him.

8

As soon as Rafiq heard the bolt of the hut being un-locked, he leaped off his sleeping mat and stood trembling. The door opened. It was still dark, and cold air poured into the stuffy interior. The boys waited, terrified.

"Get out!"

They didn't need to be told twice. They scuttled out and stood in a ragged line, shivering, bewildered, eyes thick with sleep. Their guard stood silently to one side, stroking his beard. He carried a stick and his cold flat gaze and dead expression frightened Rafiq. Abdullah marched up and down, brandishing his gun. His voice rang out clear and hard in the thin air.

"You have been brought here to train as soldiers, to learn how to fight for Kashmir's freedom. Freedom from India's rule. Freedom from oppression. Freedom from injustice.

You are true sons of Kashmir, which is why you were chosen. You are strong. You have courage. But most of all, you are proud. Proud to be Kashmiri!"

Rafiq listened. He remembered his father telling him that being Indian made him hold his head high, but being Kashmiri made his heart beat and his blood shine. Abdullah continued.

"Work hard, learn well and you will succeed. To succeed is to become a soldier of the Kashmiri freedom fighters, fighting the war for your country, making your people proud." He dropped his voice low. "But if you are weak, if you are a coward, and if you ever try to escape, you will fail. And if you fail, you will die like a dog!"

The words were shocking. Rafiq thought of the boy gunned down in the desert for trying to escape. Abdullah's voice rose with fervour as he strode back and forth in front of the boys.

"Your training begins today, in these mountains. Success brings great reward, both now and in the afterlife. It is an honour to be chosen. Never forget that! We are soldiers of Kashmir. We will fight and we will be free, but we need new blood. New blood to free our people. New blood to fight the enemy. You are our new blood!"

Rafiq felt his heart beat faster, thumping against his ribcage, as he listened. Spit flew from Abdullah's mouth; his face was flushed. He was shouting and flinging his arms in the air, swinging his gun towards the sky.

"We are proud people and will not be broken. God

instructs us to fight for the people of our country, in the name of Kashmir, in the name of Allah. We will destroy the enemy that seeks to oppress us. And the children of the enemy. And their children's children. Together we will make Kashmir free!"

Abdullah fired his rifle in the air, once, twice, three times, and the bearded guard cheered. The reports cracked open the morning. Abdullah's voice dropped low again as the smoke cleared.

"Training is hard but you must *never* give in, even when you are hurting. To give in is weakness. To give in is cowardice. To give in is shameful. Obey us quickly and in the name of Allah." His voice dropped to little more than a whisper. "Or you will not survive."

Rafiq thought back to a time when his father had taken him to see freedom fighters demonstrating against Indian rule in his village. Angry men with their faces masked had marched down the street, shouting and firing guns and rockets into the air.

"Is it right what they are doing?" Rafiq had asked his father.

"It is always right to seek freedom from oppression, Rafiq," his father had told him. "Freedom is every man's greatest gift. If you are not free, then you are nothing. But there are right ways and wrong ways to gain your freedom."

The Indian army had arrived all the way from Srinagar and beaten back the demonstrators, dragging men away. The crowds had got angrier, spitting at the police and screaming. Blood had been spilled. Rafiq's father had pulled his small son away from the danger, back to the safety of their home. The next day, Rafiq and his friends had gone to look at the brown stains in the dirt, poking at them with sticks and imitating the chanting until local shopkeepers had thrown stones to chase them away.

It seemed so long ago, so far away, but Rafiq still remembered his father's words:

"Our religion is one of peace, Rafiq. It disagrees with hurting and killing innocent people. A war is between one military force and another, never attacking or harming innocent people. Allah does not wish us to destroy lives."

Rafiq was confused. How could Allah's will be so different here in the mountains? For now, he decided, it was wiser to forget Allah's wishes and listen to Abdullah's instead, for it seemed that his word must be obeyed.

Abdullah split the boys into two groups. "You are collecting fuel," he told one group, and to the bearded guard, "Kareem, they're yours."

Wordlessly Kareem strolled over and cuffed the nearest boy hard on the ear, pointing towards the outline of the hills. The boy flinched and, with a sob, started running towards them. Kareem moved to the next boy, who didn't wait for the blow but took off straight away. The whole group followed, sprinting towards the hills, while Kareem walked behind them, his dead face expressionless.

An old man appeared, clattering from behind the screened-off cooking area, knees bowed beneath a towering stack of old buckets, which he dumped noisily on the ground in front of them.

"Fill the water containers," Abdullah ordered the second group, pointing towards the river with his gun. "Go! Go! Go!"

The frightened children grabbed a couple of buckets each and dashed towards the river, tumbling and falling down the hillside in their haste to follow orders.

"Get a move on! Shift yourselves. Faster! Faster!" shouted the old man, swinging a heavy stick as they passed him.

Everything had to be done at a run in the mountains. Rafiq found himself scurrying, tripping, plummeting down the slope to the mist-wreathed black water, where he waded in and dunked his buckets. He hauled them out and began struggling back up the hill, his arms straining from the weight, sweat beading on his brow in spite of the chill morning. Abdullah swung a kick at the boys as they scuttled past. The old man swiped at their legs with his stick, cracking them on their shins and calves.

"Get used to it. Focus. Take the pain," he yelled at them.

One boy stumbled as the stick caught him on the ankle. Water slopped out. Abdullah lifted his rifle and jabbed it hard into the boy's ribs.

"Fool!" he spat, and the boy cried out and crumpled over, clutching his injured side. The two buckets crashed to the ground, water spilling out and seeping into the parched earth.

"Weakness is apparent already!" Abdullah screamed at him. "Toughen up or you'll never be a soldier."

He grabbed the child's upper arm, lifted him clear off the ground and threw him back onto the stony surface. He picked up the two buckets and clattered them on top of the boy's shivering body. Rafiq and the others paused to stare. Instantly the old man was there, slamming his stick down on their backs.

"Get on with your work," he shouted at them. "Or you'll join him in the dirt."

They hurried on, tipping the water into large jars in the cooking area before returning for another run. As Rafiq scrambled down a second time, he met the injured boy coming back up. His face was pale and his walk was slow, painful. His buckets were only half full and he stooped over, grimacing with each step. Water slopped out and ran down his legs. Rafiq was too scared to help and passed without a word.

Once the jars were full, they gathered in front of their huts, waiting for the next order, their eyes darting from Abdullah to the old man, trying to anticipate any kicks or punches.

"Wash before prayers," Abdullah commanded and away they ran to the river for a third time to cleanse themselves.

From over the hill Kareem's group came scurrying, their arms full of dried animal dung, twigs and broken sticks, which they heaped next to the fire. Then they too came tumbling down the slope to the river, several with bloody noses and bruised lips. The boys washed quickly and silently, until the old man croaked and lifted his stick, and they immediately ran back to the compound for prayers.

Afterwards there was no eating, although the women were frying eggs and roasting chapattis on pans over the fire. The aroma made Rafiq's mouth water. Milk tea bubbled in a pot and the spicy fragrance of cardamom brought to his mind images of his mother preparing breakfast. His daydream was cut short by Abdullah's voice.

"Go! Quickly."

And the kidnapped boys were marched into the mountains, climbing steep slopes and crossing goat trails until they came to a place that was flat and smooth. Rocks had been cleared away from the hard-packed ground, which was laid out with wooden spars and logs, lashed together to make parallel bars and high ladders, barriers and low structures strung with heavy netting. Rafiq and the other boys stared in silence. They had believed the mountains to be wild and empty.

Abdullah pointed. "Every boy will complete this assault course in ten minutes. If one fails, nobody gets food."

Rafiq felt his stomach tighten. He glanced at the boys around him and knew the weak ones who would struggle. He felt resentful towards them already.

Kareem squatted silently on a large boulder like a vulture, watching, while the old man marched them through the course, rapidly explaining what they must climb over, crawl under and swing from. Rafiq listened closely, feeling a spark of excitement in his belly at the challenge ahead. He was good at sports in school. Fast and strong. He revised in his mind the brief instructions as they returned to the start.

The old man pulled out a stopwatch and a whistle, which he blasted for each boy to begin, and away they went, climbing and struggling. It was confusing and exhausting. Uncertain what to clamber over or scramble under, they were afraid to stop, throwing every scrap of energy into running, leaping, jumping. Abdullah prowled among them, screaming and hitting out. He kicked any boy who fell, until he crawled away or laboured to his feet again. The old man wrote down everyone's time in a grubby notebook. Kareem remained at a distance, but missed nothing.

When Rafiq's turn came, he took off like a bullet, pushing himself relentlessly. He wheezed and panted, the thin air scarcely enough to satisfy his gasping lungs. He tore through the course, then sprinted back to the start.

Abdullah ordered them to do it again. The whistle blasted and they were off again before they even had time to catch their breath.

By the time it came to the third circuit, Rafiq was exhausted. His muscles were fatigued and he had no energy. As he tried to leap from one log to another he misjudged, and his body slammed against the rough wood. He groaned and slithered to the ground, cracking his jaw on the timber, doubling over when he hit the dirt. He had bitten his tongue and spat out blood.

Instantly Abdullah was there, looming over him, yelling, punching, dragging him up by the collar.

"Again!" he bawled, beating Rafiq across the back of the head with his hand. "Do it again."

Rafiq tried, but fell again, flopping foolishly to the ground. He felt weak with hunger and exhaustion. He wiped his sleeve across his bloody mouth. Abdullah hauled him to his feet a second time.

"You will not give up. Show strength. Control your body. Again!"

Rafiq stood a little unsteadily, his head spinning. His arms hurt and his belly was empty. He could hear boys grunting and panting; Abdullah was shouting and ranting in his face. The sun dazzled him. He clenched his jaw and gritted his teeth and glared at the log. His fists were hard as rocks. He kept staring until all other distractions faded away. All he could see was the log he had to leap onto. It wasn't going to get the better of him. He was Rafiq: strong and able. He hadn't been the youngest chosen for nothing.

He tightened his muscles and leaped, grabbing the log with his arms, twisting his legs around it and hauling himself over until he dropped down on the other side. For a second, his deep frown faded. In spite of everything, he allowed himself a quick grin of satisfaction. And he glanced back briefly to check that Abdullah had witnessed his achievement.

The old man finally blew the whistle and the boys at the finishing line collapsed in an exhausted heap. The only boy yet to finish was the one whom Abdullah had thrown on the ground that morning for slopping water. He was painfully slow and dragged himself round the assault course, still holding on to his side even though it was hours since he'd been beaten. Rafiq anxiously watched Abdullah in case he decided to starve them all. Finally Rafiq could bear it no longer.

"Hurry up," he yelled at the boy, kicking the dirt in frustration.

The others looked at him in astonishment. How could he turn on one of their own? But when the injured boy still dragged himself along, they shouted too, yelling at him to go harder, faster.

"Stop slacking! Get moving!"

"We want food."

"Try harder!"

When the boy stumbled and fell, which seemed to happen at just about every obstacle, Rafiq picked up a stone like the gunman had the previous day when he had been frozen on the rocks. He swung his arm and hurled it through the air, aiming at the boy's head so that the sting would get him moving faster. The stone cracked against its target and the boy started crying, bent almost double as he limped along.

After a moment of initial discomfort the other boys again followed Rafiq's actions, and small missiles zipped through the air like a swarm of wasps, spattering the ground with tiny explosions of dust. When the boy eventually lurched across the line and fell on the ground, the old man blew his whistle. Then, to their great relief, he rooted deeply in his canvas bag and handed out rounds of chapattis and hard-boiled eggs. Rafiq grabbed the food, right from the fist of an older boy who didn't expect it, and scuttled off to one side to wolf it down.

"Do you want water?" Abdullah asked them.

They looked at him, uncertain whether or not they should reply. He pointed to the next hill.

"There are five bottles of water over there. The first five boys back here with a bottle can drink it."

Lifting his rifle, he fired into the air. The boys were growing accustomed to the sound of gunfire and hardly flinched. Instead they started sprinting, tumbling down the slope. They all wanted water.

Rafiq ran as fast as he could. Even so, several older boys pulled ahead, swiftly reaching the large boulders scattered on the far hillside. They started scrambling over them, but Rafiq was quicker and lighter. Once he reached the boulders, he made up the distance, squeezing through gaps that the bigger boys had to climb over or around. He passed one, two, three boys. Only two ahead of him now, and there were five bottles of water. The two boys in front were teenagers who moved swiftly. Rafiq couldn't catch them but he kept his lead on the others and concentrated on the rocks ahead. His breathing was laboured, his chest bursting from the effort, his mouth dry. At one point he got jammed in a tight crevice between two large rocks. Panic rose as he clawed himself out, skinning his knees.

He reached the top of the hill. The two lead runners snatched up bottles from the small pile. Rafiq grabbed his water, pleased with himself, and stashed it inside his shirt.

Dropping down through the rocks was easier than climbing up. He skimmed over loose shale and slid through gaps. As he was emerging from between two large boulders, a shadow flitted past. Rafiq just had time to turn, when a dark shape dropped down on him from above. It was another boy. The two of them tumbled in a jumble of arms and legs, rolling through the dirt. They came to a jarring stop against a rock and fought to free themselves. Stunned, Rafiq sat up, pushing the boy away from him.

"What are you—?" he began, but the boy smashed him on the side of the head with a rock. Then he was off and gone. Rafiq lifted his hand to his temple and winced with pain. His head was pounding. He was confused and shocked. Struggling to his feet, he felt for his water bottle.

It was gone. His attacker had stolen it. The other boy hadn't even bothered climbing the rocks, but had lain in wait and then ambushed him to steal his water.

Rafiq strode back to where the rest of the group were gathered, his face dark, anger crackling through his blood. He could see the thief jubilantly swigging from the snatched water bottle. Rafiq stormed over to him, boys quickly clearing out of the way. They looked anxiously at their captors, who did nothing but watch. Abdullah even had a smirk smeared on his face. Rafiq stopped in front of the thief, swung his arm back and punched the other boy in the stomach. He gasped and dropped to the ground, doubled over. The water bottle spun away, its contents leaking into the sand. Rafiq turned to walk away but jerked to a stop when Kareem blocked his path.

"He took my water," Rafiq spluttered. "I got it first. He stole it from me."

Without warning, Kareem lifted his arm and hit Rafiq hard. Pain exploded through him and he crumpled to the ground, unable to breathe. Kareem spat in the dirt next to him.

"That's for being stupid enough to let him," he replied.

9

Every evening, after the sun had gone down but when the air still held on to the golden dust of daylight, Jameela lit the kerosene lamp and placed it in the brass holder next to Rafiq's cot. She liked the light of the flickering flame as it shone through the woven curtains. It was easier to imagine that Rafiq was on the other side of the rough weave fabric, and he seemed closer to her than at other times during the day. He was in her thoughts at every waking moment, but most of all just after sunset, when he used to come home from the mosque. Jameela would bring him lemon tea because she knew he liked it.

It had been many months since the boys had been seized, but still no one had managed to find any trace of them. The day following the kidnapping, the police had arrived from Varahamula in a long important line of cars filled with boxes of papers and documents, rubber stamps and fold-up chairs, small wooden desks and typewriters. They moved into the few houses in the village that had rooms to spare, some of them even sleeping in the haunted cots and on the mats of the lost boys. Other villagers sent bowls of food each evening. The police closed the school for a week and set up their heaps of official inquiry paraphernalia there.

Jameela went to the school with her parents, queuing with the other bereft families to make their reports to the police. The building was crowded. Typewriters tapped and rattled all day. The yard was full of families waiting to be seen, sitting or squatting in the sun.

Jameela spent a long time staring at the chalk line that was still faintly visible on the wall of the classroom. Although she had seen it before, it haunted her. It was smudged and grubby from the hands of all the villagers who had touched and lingered over it. The police took photographs of it and measured its height from the floor of the classroom. The little children waiting with their families measured themselves against it, pleased that they weren't yet tall enough to reach the line.

Mahmood jumped up to measure himself.

"Sit down," his papa warned sharply.

Mahmood ran and threw himself in his mother's lap, hiding his face. When his father's attention wasn't on him any more, he wandered over to the wall and poked his fingers into the holes left by the militants' bullets.

It was late afternoon when they were called in. The police officer taking their report sat at a desk too small for him. His legs were pressed tightly together and his knees were jammed beneath it. He looked very uncomfortable. Jameela could see great patches of sweat under his arms and there were trickles running down the side of his face. Sitting on the desk were a small typewriter and a stack of coloured forms. The officer took a white form, a green form, a blue form and a pink form. He then took three sheets of carbon paper and placed them between each of the four forms, putting the white form on the top. These he threaded carefully onto the roller of the typewriter and adjusted the bars to accommodate the pages.

"Boy's name?" he asked.

"Rafiq." Jameela's father gave the answers.

"Family name?"

The officer had to take time to find each letter on the typewriter before he punched it down methodically.

"Address?"

After he had typed two lines, he scrolled the paper up a little and checked that the carbon paper was working properly and that the coloured forms were correctly aligned so that the typing appeared in the right boxes. He seemed satisfied with his work and they continued.

"Date of birth of the boy?"

Jameela's father gave the date. The police officer paused for a moment, then counted carefully on his fingers. He looked up.

"The birth year must be wrong," he said. "That makes him only nine."

Jameela's father slid his eldest son's birth certificate from an envelope and showed the police officer. "My son was only nine years old."

The officer shook his head. "I have a son of nine years also. I'm sorry for your loss."

They worked their way through a long list of official questions. It took for ever to get everything down. Once the form was finished, the officer took it out and read over it carefully. He took it over to a desk where another police official sat with a rubber stamp and a pen. Each completed form was read slowly by this second official, who stamped the police stamp on each of the four pages, signed it with a squiggle and handed it back to the typing officer, who returned to the family. The officer filed the forms in separate baskets, except the pink one, which he handed to Jameela's father.

"You keep this one," he told them.

After a week in the school with their coloured forms and official furniture and rubber stamps, the police headed back through the mountains to Varahamula, glad to have the job finished. They left the villagers with a pink form in place of each stolen child and promises to return once there was news. School opened up again and lessons resumed for those left behind. One teacher had to leave because he had no children to teach. One of the classrooms was permanently empty. The school football team was dissolved because there were no longer enough players.

The limited news that did come back from the police

was not good. The body of a boy was found on one of the remote roads leading to the mountains, about six or seven hours from the village. Peppered with bullet holes, half eaten by rats and birds, dried by the sun, it lay beneath a sagging heap of torn and dirty cloth until a camel train led by traders crossing the desert found it and told the authorities in the next town.

The small collection of bones and rags and clumps of hair was brought back to the village. Identification was impossible and the dead child was buried, mourned by almost twenty grieving families, who gathered together to share their tears. Each family hoped that the murdered boy was the child of their neighbour. After the burial they waited in a state of high anxiety, thinking that perhaps the bodies of murdered boys would be found at intervals, littered around the countryside. But no more dead children were discovered. No more news came either.

When they went to Varahamula to buy their kerosene and rice and cloth, the villagers called at the police station and were told that the case was still open. Still under investigation. Still active. But the weeks stretched into months and no more information came.

The fathers went back to their work and the mothers cooked the food and cared for their remaining children. On the surface, life in the village returned to normal. Grief was shut behind the walls of homes and locked into hearts that had no known deaths to mourn, no hurt bodies to weep over, no sons to welcome home.

But every night in Jameela's home, when the family meal was over and they gathered in the evening light of the courtyard, as was their custom, the conversation inevitably turned to Rafiq.

"It's boring now Rafiq isn't here," Mahmood said one evening.

"I'll play with you," Jameela offered, although she didn't particularly enjoy the kind of running and climbing games he liked to play.

To her relief Mahmood's expression made it clear how little he thought of her suggestion. Instead he clambered into the lower branches of the walnut tree and hung upside down, observing the goings-on from this new angle. Afrah danced beneath him, stretching her arms to touch his fingertips.

"I wonder who he plays chase with now," he continued, flickering his fingers at the laughing toddler. "And if he's still playing football." His voice had a bit of a sulk in it.

"Your brother may not be playing with anyone," his mother said sadly, rocking a sleepy Imraan in her lap. "Now get down before you fall and crack your head on the ground."

Mahmood pulled a face as he swung upright and sat on the branch instead.

Jameela had brought out Rafiq's school bag. Slowly she undid the buckle and slid out the books Rafiq had been using to teach her reading. She opened one of them and stared at her brother's writing, tracing her finger over the shapes, feeling where the paper was indented from his pencil.

"It's time for prayer," her father said, turning to leave.

Jameela knew this time was hardest for him, because it had previously been shared with Rafiq. She lifted her face to smile but he was not looking at her. Instead he stopped and stared at the book on her lap. Jameela looked down, blushing, but when she peeked up, he was striding out of the courtyard.

"Is it wrong to look at Rafiq's books, Mamma?" she whispered as soon as he had gone.

"No, Jameela," her mother soothed her. "What harm are you doing? But your father…" She shook her head. "He finds this all too hard. He doesn't know what to do, what to say."

"He looks at me crossly, as if I have done something bad."

"You *have* done something bad. You're not allowed to learn to read," piped up Mahmood from his perch.

"I told you to get down, Mahmood," his mother said sharply. She turned back to Jameela. "Your papa hasn't slept properly since Rafiq was taken. All night he tosses about and throws himself around, sick with worry about your brother. He doesn't mean to be sharp. It would be the same if you went missing."

Jameela nodded, but secretly she didn't think so.

Mahmood, back on the ground again, lifted the rope tied around the goat's neck.

"Shall I take her for water before bed?" he asked.

"No! That's Rafiq's job," Jameela responded quickly, jumping up.

"But he's not here."

Mahmood's words cut a knife into her heart. She busied herself by slipping the books back into the bag and brushing dust off her skirt so he would not see the tears that stung her eyes.

"Then I'll go with you," she replied softly, and they walked out together.

As she watched them leave, their mother recalled Jameela and Rafiq standing together on the last golden evening before he was stolen. The sun had been behind her two eldest children, so that their dark silhouettes were outlined with a rim of brightness. Rafiq had held the rope, the little nanny goat bleating softly. Jameela had stood looking up at him, gentle teasing fluttering between them. They had only stood still for seconds but their mother held that memory deep in her heart, treasuring it, for she didn't know if they'd ever be together again.

10

They poured into the cold misty morning in a flood of skinny brown bodies. Rafiq ran with the other boys and drew the fresh dawn air deeply into his lungs. The day was good. Ice sparkled on the rocks and glinted from the black shale. As he relieved himself at the back of the hut, he peered skywards, but even though he stretched his neck, he wasn't able to see everything of the vast expanse of the heavens spread above the settlement. He was still astonished by this view, even after a whole year of seeing it.

A rifle shot echoed in the air, signalling the start of their day, and he blinked and was off. He ran and grabbed his buckets, clattering down to the river, shivering as his bare toes crunched through the lacing of ice at the water's edge. Dip, fill, carry and empty. His arms were strong now, muscular, easily able to lift the full buckets clear of the ground, and he enjoyed this change in his body.

He did three runs, ignoring the other boys, who ran in twos and threes, chattering together. He preferred his own company. There was less chance of Kareem beating him if he put his head down and undertook his tasks quickly and quietly. He threw the containers back in the heap and returned to the sandy riverbank, where he washed with his brothers in preparation for morning prayers.

Afterwards he huddled close to the blazing fire. The old man had lit it earlier and was bent over the bright flames, boiling up a large pot of milk tea with cardamom and sugar. Rafiq watched him, feeling the scented steam damp on his cheeks. He was tired because he never slept well in this mountain home. His nights were crowded with frightening shapes and indefinable sounds, spelling out the character of his days. Sometimes he lay in the dark, afraid to shut his eyes, and listened in wonder to the deep breathing and snoring of his brothers around him. How could they sleep so peacefully?

"Are you ready for this day?" the old man asked, dipping an enamel mug into the pot of tea. "It's an important one for you."

Rafiq's stomach lurched. It was indeed an important day, but he couldn't trust himself to answer. Instead he took the scalding mug and retreated to sip its contents slowly, standing slightly apart from the rest of the group. The boy soldiers were nervous, excited. Anxiety rippled like electricity through their limbs, but Rafiq kept it inside.

On the surface he appeared calm, his quiet gaze and composed movements contradicting the turmoil and agitation that coursed through his body.

It was an important day. A day of reckoning.

"Have you seen the guns?" one boy spluttered enthusiastically, running up to Rafiq from the direction of the munitions hut and jumping around in the dirt. "Kareem is unwrapping them by the hut. They're for us! And Abdullah is taking out the mines that we'll be laying. It's real today. All real."

Rafiq looked at him derisively over the twists of steam. "This is not a game," he said sharply. "This is a day when we will be judged. Failure is not an option. Do you not realize the significance of this day?"

Abruptly the boy ceased his jumping and stared. He ought to have known better than to spill over with excitement in front of Rafiq. He was too serious, too intense, to get a thrill from today: their first real assignment. The boy pulled a face and moved away. Moments later Rafiq heard him chattering to others, their voices raised in anticipation.

They had all been preparing for this day since they had arrived at the camp, raw and terrified.

Abdullah had spoken to them about it. "This is your home now," he said as they stood silently in front of him. "We are your brothers, your family, your life. We have trained you and you are no longer soft village boys. You are almost men. Tough. Skilled. Capable of continuing this fight. But you must prove yourselves to us. You must earn the right to become free soldiers of Kashmir."

Rafiq caught his breath when he heard Abdullah speak of free soldiers; but as he continued, the meaning became clear: freedom from beatings and thrashings, freedom to join the men and older boys as they sat around the fires at night, freedom to sleep in the huts without being locked in, freedom to roam. There was no mention of freedom to return to their village.

"We will set you a challenge to test your skills. If you perform well, we will know that you are true soldiers – warriors who have not allowed physical or emotional weakness to stand in your way. True warriors are not attached to one place or one family. True warriors suffer for God. Your old families are behind you now, gone for ever. Your home is here, and your loyalty is to Allah and the cause for which we fight."

Even if it meant not returning to his village, Rafiq wanted the freedom of which Abdullah spoke. He was weary – a weariness that made his bones ache and his heart sore. He was weary of being beaten; he was weary of being punished. His legs were bruised and his feet were cut from scrambling over rocks and rough terrain. Sometimes, when he couldn't help it, he cried himself to sleep at night. He was furious with himself for this weakness, and would bury his face deep in his blanket so the other boys wouldn't hear his sobs. He missed being part of his family ... any family. He used to be somebody's brother, somebody's son, but not any more. If these men were prepared to accept him as their brother, then he wanted it. And if it meant carrying out this assignment to prove he could be one of them, then Rafiq was going to do it.

Many of the older boys at the camp had been through the same experiences as the recent recruits.

"You forget about your old family after a while," they said, laughing at the stricken faces of the raw village children. "You become a man here – fighting for God. There is no greater honour. You'll no longer be a little child from a village. When you are a man, you won't need your mamma or your papa. You'll have your brothers here, and together we are strong."

Other older boys had joined up voluntarily.

"The Indian government left my village with no food because we would not obey their curfews or hand over our money for their taxes," one boy told Rafiq when they were collecting water at the river. "My sisters died from hunger and my parents got sick. I heard about the army in the hills, fighting the government, so I joined them. I had nowhere else to go. That was three summers ago."

Rafiq looked at him. The boy was about twelve or thirteen.

"This is my family now," he went on, using the long nail on his little finger to pick wax from his ear. He examined it then flicked it away. "This is all the family I need. I am honoured to have been accepted here to fight. When you are here for longer, you will understand."

Not everyone was to participate in today's mission.

There were some boys who weren't able to learn the tactics they needed to fight a war, no matter how many times they were beaten. One or two had simply disappeared. One day they were there, struggling to keep up; the next they were gone: missing from the huts when the boys were locked in at night, or not returning from a day's training in the mountains. The others noticed, but nobody asked questions; nobody looked for them. Some weaker boys worked around the camp caring for the goats and hens, cleaning pots, fetching fuel. They would never be given more freedom and they knew it. They scurried with their buckets past where the aspiring young soldiers trained, their eyes downcast, their shoulders hunched.

"Not everyone has the strength to be a warrior," Abdullah told the selected boys as they stood around the fire on the morning of the challenge. "You are the chosen ones, those who God has decided should fight this war. It is a privilege to be selected for this task. A great honour."

Rafiq drank his tea and felt an unfamiliar feeling spread through his bones. He realized that this mission was not something into which he had been coerced; he had earned it. He had mastered new skills, had understood the tactics needed to be a warrior. His thoughts grew stronger and bigger. He lifted his head and felt taller. He thought of his father and wondered what he would say if he knew that Rafiq was the youngest to be chosen – again. His father had always told his son to strive to be the best, to do well at whatever was asked of him, to be strong in the face of adversity. Surely his father would be proud of him now?

The boy soldiers left the encampment before dawn had fully stained the sky. Each carried heavy packs, an AK-47 and bullets strapped around his body. They walked across the hills, cutting past high goat trails, along a route they had not followed before. Kareem led the way, his gun slung over his shoulder; Abdullah was at the rear. Two older boys came with them as extra scouts on the mission; they were experienced soldiers, accustomed to fighting. There was no talk as they tramped over the rough terrain. They sweated heavily, but this was part of the test: did they have the stamina to be good soldiers? Nobody complained. There were no whiners in this group.

Their route was a solitary one, and although they saw a cluster of small mountain huts in the distance, the occupants would not have seen the boys, who were careful not to crest the skyline. By the time they reached the dirt road, their final destination, it was still early in the day, although they had been walking for several hours. Concealing their packs in a ditch, they gathered around Abdullah and Kareem and hunkered low, out of sight of the road.

"You'll work in pairs," Abdullah told them. "Each pair is to set and position mines on the road, in a figure of five configuration as if preparing to take out a large vehicle."

He distributed shovels, picks and unarmed landmines.

"Don't arm your mines," he warned. "This is an exercise."

The group was split in two. Half was sent further up

the road with Kareem and one scout. Rafiq remained behind and was paired with an older boy called Ahmed. They sized each other up. Rafiq had not worked closely with Ahmed before and, although he knew him to be a capable trainee, had never spoken to him. The only thing he had noticed was that he was always smiling, which Rafiq found hard to understand, since he could see nothing to be happy about. Ahmed, for his part, looked at Rafiq and saw a strong boy with dark serious eyes. He knew Rafiq as the tough and determined trainee who kept apart from the group and always looked like he'd just heard the world was about to end. In fact, Ahmed had never seen Rafiq smile.

Their scout escorted them down the road, where they were to lay mines. They'd done it many times before, first in the dirt around the encampment with stones as mines and sticks as guns, then with wooden discs and cut-out timber guns on the goat trails snaking through the mountains. This time they had real weapons.

"Do you want to dig or shall I?" Ahmed asked, cradling the mine in his hands. He was grinning.

Rafiq stared at him. "I'll dig," he replied and immediately began to count his paces to locate the mine accurately.

"I'll cover you from the ditch, then position and conceal," Ahmed said.

Rafiq located the sweet spot to set the mine. It was easy because the road was deeply rutted from the wheels of passing vehicles, but he remembered that this was a test and carefully paced out the distance from the centre of the road. He started to dig while Ahmed hid in the ditch, cradling the precious mine, his AK-47 propped upright beside him. The earth was hard packed and solid, forcing Rafiq to loosen the surface with the pick before he could lift any out. This was going to take longer than he had expected and he felt exposed and vulnerable. If this were a real mission, he would be easily taken out by the enemy. He glanced towards the ditch, doubting that Ahmed had the focus needed to cover him properly or watch for snipers.

"That's deep enough. Deep enough!" Ahmed hissed when Rafiq had dug a shallow depression.

Rafiq ignored him. Ahmed was not in charge and Rafiq would decide for himself. He fiddled around for a bit longer, scratching the hard clay and smoothing the sides of the hole.

"That's too deep," Ahmed spluttered. "Fill it up a bit."

When Rafiq was satisfied with his work, he retreated to the ditch, keeping low and alert, watching for potential snipers hidden among the rocks. He retrieved his gun and lay prone before giving any attention to Ahmed.

"Go and set your mine, Ahmed," Rafiq ordered quietly.

Ahmed looked at him and, without a word, climbed onto the road, holding the mine carefully. He gently lowered it into the hole, where it fitted perfectly. Looking back at Rafiq, he pointed.

"Perfect fit!" he mouthed.

Rafiq ignored him. Of course it was a perfect fit.

Ahmed scooped earth over it, a branch laid on the ground beside him, ready to brush the earth and conceal his presence once his work was complete. All around, the other boys were laying their mines, concentrating on their work and watching for snipers as they had been taught to do.

Even though he was watching, Rafiq wasn't prepared for the huge bus that appeared without warning round the sharp bend. There was a wind in his ears so the noise of the wheels tearing into the dirt was not audible. There was no sound of gears straining, even on the steep incline. The roar of its engine was muffled behind the hump of the mountain.

Suddenly it was there, thundering and lumbering and huge, heading straight for Ahmed, who was bent over, brushing the switch across the dirt covering the landmine. He had his back to the bus. Rafiq screamed at him and ducked down into the ditch, crouching as low as he could.

The empty mountain broke out of its silence and erupted with noise and shouts and screeching brakes and clouds of dust. Gravel spat from beneath the wheels that halted just above Rafiq's head, stinging his chest and face. Then Ahmed was there beside him, slithering in on a rake of gravel, his absurd grin emerging from behind the dirt and the fright. The scout was there too, slipping and sliding into the dry ditch.

"Hide your guns," he hissed. "Quick, quick! Up the mountain. Get out of here."

He jabbed Rafiq hard in the ribs with the muzzle of his gun and they were away, scuttling up towards a steep rocky pass. Ahmed leaped past on long legs, grabbing Rafiq's shirt and half dragging him along. They stumbled and fell on the shale, slithering back down in a wild knot of limbs, but were up and running again in an instant.

Behind him Rafiq heard voices but was afraid to look. Abdullah – or worse, Kareem – might be right behind him and the beating he would receive wasn't worth it. He felt panic rise in his chest as he realized that the bus might have been part of the test. It must have been expected. Abdullah and Kareem must have known when it was due. Yet Rafiq hadn't been ready for it. He'd been watching for snipers in the hills – the flash of sunlight on a gun, the quick movement of a dark head emerging from a dun background – but he'd never expected a thundering vehicle. Rafiq dreaded to think how Kareem and Abdullah would punish them.

They were out of breath when they finally stopped, high above the road, nearly up at the pass. Rafiq leaned over, his hands on his knees, and gasped for air. All of the boys were high up the hill by now, scattered across its flank, having raced up from where they'd been working on the road. Abdullah and Kareem were close, checking the area. Rafiq studied their faces and was relieved to see from Abdullah's expression that the bus was as much of a surprise to him as it had been to the boys. Kareem was muttering furiously about Indian bus timetables.

They all looked down towards the road, where the bus, now small and far away, was moving off. The panic was over. They stood and watched as it gathered speed. There were faces at the windows, gazing up at the distant figures. It looked like the bus that went through Rafiq's village.

Watching it drive away stirred memories that he had not gone near for a long time: of travelling to market with his father, or with his mother and little Jameela.

But Rafiq's thoughts were interrupted by a loud curse from Abdullah. He spat on the ground and mumbled something to Kareem, who began descending once again, his face dark, his stick swinging in his hand. Rafiq flinched, instantly afraid. He looked towards the road in a panic in case he had forgotten to do something; in case he was the reason for the sudden rage.

But there was something else visible on the road.

A boy. One of their group. Rafiq recognized him from the sleeping hut. He had climbed out of the ditch and was staring at the back of the retreating bus. He just stood there in the middle of the road. Not moving, just staring. Rafiq guessed this boy too had recognized the bus and his memories were coming out of their hiding place.

Only when the bus was gone did the boy react. He ran after it, sprinting fast along the dirt road, waving his thin arms above his head and screaming. Screaming for them to come back, to please come back for him. To please take him home. His small voice echoed in the hills, twisted around the rocks, lost itself in the vastness of the mountains.

But it was too late. The bus had gone, thundering along its meandering route with its load of village people and vegetables and ordinary things.

And where it had come from was no longer the boys' home.

11

One clear bright morning, almost a year after Rafiq was taken, Jameela and her mother left their house, rushing for the bus that would take them to town to sell their goods and buy essential provisions. Jameela carried Imraan and a basket of walnuts from their tree. Her mother was laden down with rolls of spun wool and a box of eggs.

"We might not make it," she worried as they hurried down the street. It had been such a rush to get Mahmood off to school and Afrah dropped at a neighbour's house for the day. They ran across the surfaced road leading to Vara-hamula, relieved to see a small group of people waiting at the far side.

"We're fine," Jameela said, looking in the distance for the dust cloud that signalled the vehicle's approach. "I can't even see it yet."

They dumped their goods at their feet and caught their breath.

"We must buy some wicks," her mother said, thinking through the long list of items they needed at home. "Don't forget we've to get your father's new prayer mat. And a new hijab for you."

"And some cotton cloth for Afrah and Mahmood," Jameela added. "They are getting so big. I'll help to stitch some clothes."

The sun was well over the houses, washing away the shadows and bleaching the ground, when the bus eventually arrived. It was more packed than usual and the villagers grumbled loudly to the driver about the crowd and the late arrival. There were chickens and ducklings in baskets down the centre aisle, a goat and its kid trussed up in a sack at a woman's feet, their heads poking out of the top, and large bags of corn stuffed beneath the seats. Crates of vegetables and rolls of wool were tied on the roof, alongside an unfortunate sheep sharing a bit of space with a bicycle. Jameela and her mother squeezed on. A woman in a front seat lifted her little boy onto her lap and made room for Jameela's mother. Pushing past the animals, Jameela carried Imraan further down the bus, where women in the back row squashed up to make space.

The bus stopped at other villages and more people crammed on, standing in the aisle and sitting on the steps at the door. Bartering and bargaining were conducted throughout the journey. Deals were struck and agreements shaken on.

Jameela looked out at the vast expanse of dry barren land. As the road climbed into the mountains, the temperature dropped sharply and the bus groaned and creaked as it struggled upwards. She could see frost sparkling in the dark shadows where the sun hadn't reached. They passed glacial lakes, green and deep, and a few mountain children from isolated hill tribes, with wind-burnt faces and small herds of goats. They wore thick woollen shawls and felt slippers, and stared at the bus as it passed.

The land became stark and stony and the bus teetered round narrow hairpin bends, slipping on loose gravel at the edges of the dirt road and passing towering cliffs and sheer drops. Jameela craned her neck to see the white-iced peaks of the Pir Panjals stretching almost as high as the sky, but they were lost in a blue haze.

They rounded a corner. Without warning, the driver of the bus jammed on the brakes. There was a mad slithering along gravel and a frightening lurch to one side. The vehicle screeched to a halt. Men and women shrieked in terror. Babies and children started to howl. Carrots and onions tumbled off the roof and rolled onto the ground.

Jameela shot forward in her seat and then back abruptly, momentarily squashing Imraan between her and the seat in front. He woke with a start and joined lustily in the cacophony, while Jameela's head smacked against the glass behind her. She grunted with the shock. Her stash of walnuts clattered over and skittered down the aisle, beneath everyone's feet. Apart from the baby's howling, there was a sudden shocked silence. The driver stood up from his seat, raking his hands through his hair.

"Oh my goodness, oh my goodness," he cried. "Look! Look out there." He pointed. They all looked. "Boys and men all over the road. Crawling in the dirt like rats. What's this all about? They're lucky to be alive. *We're* lucky to be alive! We could have been killed."

Jameela jiggled Imraan on her knee to try to calm him, but that only resulted in his vomiting his breakfast all over her and crying even louder. She mopped up as best she could and rocked him more gently, soothing him with soft words, while the door of the bus opened. The driver and some passengers jumped out to investigate. There was a great commotion. Jameela craned her neck to see what was happening.

After a short while they returned to the bus. There was little chat, but everyone watched their faces, read their movements. They were plainly anxious to move on, to clear out of the area. The engine throbbed to life and the bus shuddered. The driver revved the accelerator, released the brake and they lurched off. Once they were on their way, whispers flew around of what had happened.

"Those strangers were up to something very odd," one man said. "We saw young boys with guns."

"They ran away up the mountain as soon as they saw us," added another.

"What were they doing?" somebody asked.

"Crouched on the ground digging holes," the first man replied. "Very strange – high up here where there is nothing."

"Only bandits and tribal settlements around," said the first man. "It's not safe to travel through at any time. It is better to keep going."

Jameela listened as she looked out of the window up the steep slopes to where the strangers had disappeared. She could just about see them in the distance, tiny figures moving away, some with faces turned down towards the departing bus. Jameela twisted round in her seat and stared back at the portion of road on which they had been working. She could see the disturbed earth, some shallow holes.

And a small figure, climbing up out of the ditch.

Jameela blinked and looked again. He was fully visible now, standing in the middle of the road, just a young boy no more than ten or eleven years old. He was staring after the bus. Jameela couldn't take her eyes off him. She felt a sudden rush of blood to her cheeks and her scalp tingled. Then the bus rounded the next hairpin bend and he was gone from view.

"Strange to see that child on his own like that," one of the village women sitting beside Jameela commented. She too was staring back along the road. "Didn't look like he belonged up here at all. Not one of the tribal people."

But Jameela couldn't answer. She felt numb. Imraan

started fidgeting in her lap, and after a moment, she faced forward again, her thoughts awhirl. Had she known that boy? Had it been Rafiq? She couldn't be certain, but her breathing quickened and her blood hummed and she couldn't wait until they arrived in town and she could tell her mother what she had seen.

"How I wish you were right, Jameela," her mother said sadly as they dragged the rolls of spun wool off the bus. "But how would my Rafiq get up there? Into the Pir Panjals, where no normal person can survive the cruel conditions?"

"I know what I saw, Mamma," Jameela insisted. "I can't say it was Rafiq, but there was a boy standing in the middle of the road. I wasn't the only one to see him. The women from the other village did too. They said he looked out of place."

Her mother sighed. "Perhaps you are right," she said, heaving up the wool. "Maybe it was one of our snatched boys. But there is nothing we can do. We can't go into those mountains and start searching. And there is no one to do it for us."

They loaded the wool, eggs and other bits and pieces onto a flat wooden wheelbarrow pushed by an old man with the scrawniest legs Jameela had ever seen, and made their way to the market.

12

Rafiq stood frozen as Kareem walked back down to the dirt road. All he could do was watch. His stomach felt as though a cold stone were in it and his hands sweated so the gun slipped through his fingers until the butt rested softly on the ground.

Kareem walked slowly and deliberately down the steep mountainside. He didn't run or sprint after the boy, who had disappeared now round a twist in the road, but stayed slow and calm. Once on the level, he turned and followed the boy. Watching him from up high, Rafiq felt his stomach sicken and his legs tremble. Kareem vanished from sight round the corner. Abdullah's voice made Rafiq jump.

"Follow Kareem," he snapped. "You will learn a lesson from this."

Rafiq lurched after Abdullah as he led them back down to the road. He was clearly furious, muttering under his breath. He clenched and unclenched his fists as he stormed down the hill, his heavy steps sinking deep into the sandy surface. Rafiq was frightened of both men but Abdullah's temper was easier to understand. Kareem's coldness chilled him to the bone.

When they had descended to the road and rounded the corner, they could see the boy in the distance. He had stopped running and was now on his knees in the dirt, gazing in the direction of the bus, a tiny figure in the middle of a deserted road. There was nothing else around; he was completely alone. There was no point in his running any further, because there was nowhere to run.

Kareem was still walking slowly, closer to him now. Abdullah, still muttering and growling with rage, had the boys marching at a smart pace and they had almost caught up. Rafiq ran a few steps, then walked again. His gun felt heavy. He glanced towards the boy, crumpled on the ground, and saw him struggle awkwardly to his feet. As he turned, Rafiq saw his expression and halted, jolted by the despair in the boy's face. It was as if something inside the boy had gone with the bus, leaving him empty. Snot and dirt streaked his face. Tears ran down his chin. He lifted his arms and gripped his head in his hands, rocking it back and forth.

Rafiq didn't want to look any more, because he didn't want to see something that might be lurking inside himself. He hugged his gun close and sprinted to catch up. He remembered that he was a soldier with a strong spirit.

This boy was weak and brought shame on his brothers.

The boy raised his distracted eyes and saw Kareem and, further back, Abdullah and the boys coming towards him. He stopped rocking his head. Slowly his thoughts came back to where he was. He glanced around at the high mountain tops, the long dirt road, the stony ditch. He looked at the boys as they got closer. The bleakness in his face was replaced with fear. He started backing away, moving along the road again but slowly now. He began to cry, but not like the loud screaming plea he'd uttered when the bus had driven away. This was more of a whimper, a soft sobbing. He stumbled over the loose stones on the road and went down on his back.

Kareem reached him first. Without a word, he lifted his stick and swung it down hard on the side of the boy's head. The boy didn't even lift his arms to protect his face.

Abdullah shouted, "Stop!" Kareem paused in the beating. "Leave him be."

Rafiq whipped round to stare in astonishment at Abdullah. Was he going to be merciful?

"We will take him with us," Abdullah said. "Nothing will happen out here. There could be more vehicles."

The boy lay on the ground, curled up like an infant, his eyes glazed. His whimpering had stopped but his face was wet with tears and blood from where Kareem had hit him. Rafiq thought he looked pathetic.

"Tie his arms behind his back and a rope around his neck. And his ankles so he cannot run."

Wordlessly they pulled the boy to his feet and coiled rope around his small wrists.

"I'm sorry," he muttered as he slumped and let the boys bind him. "I just want to go home. I saw my people on that bus. I want to go back to my village," he sobbed. "I dream of going back to my village. Don't you dream the same?"

Rafiq concentrated on tightening the knot around his ankles, keeping his face down, but his heart was hurting as he listened. He wanted to cry, but he was a soldier and these were not the thoughts of a soldier. So he hardened his heart and shut his ears and did what he was required to do. When they had tied him up, Kareem took the rope around the boy's neck and held him as if he were an animal on a leash.

"Finish the task you came to do," he told the rest of them.

They trailed miserably back to the half-set mines and picked up their abandoned tools. Ahmed took his switch and continued brushing the dry soil across the freshly filled hole. Abdullah appeared at his side.

"Uncover the mine, check its depth for successful operation and then fully arm it."

Rafiq looked up, taken aback, but said not a word. This was new. They had been told not to arm the mines, that it was just an exercise, a mission to assess the boys' skills.

"That bus won't be back for hours," Ahmed said as he worked. "It's not the target. The freedom fighters don't hit village buses. There must be a military convoy or government vehicle coming. Maybe a bus on its way to a religious festival. We're only interested in Indian targets, not Kashmiri market buses."

Once the mine was uncovered, Rafiq scuttled from the ditch and knelt on the road. He removed the safety clip and armed the device. Gently he smoothed clay and small stones on top. They could just glimpse the gleam of the pressure plate through the light covering of soil. The scout returned to check their work.

"Now we leave," he told them.

They collected their packs and tools and headed back over the hills, climbing the steep slope yet again. Kareem was dragging their broken boy prisoner by his neck rope. He had shortened it so the boy had to walk stooped all the time, like an animal. Rafiq couldn't bear to look at him. He kept his eyes down. They climbed to the top and took a new route to the west.

"Move away from the point of attack as soon as your work is finished," Abdullah told them, an instruction they had heard a hundred times before. "Keep your needs at bay. Tiredness, hunger, thirst: these are distractions you must suppress when fighting a war. What you suffer, you suffer for Allah."

The sun had moved across the sky and shadows had begun to squat beneath the rocks when they stopped in an unfamiliar valley. They put down their packs and took out food and water: bread pancakes, potatoes, sweet bananas. The water bottles were passed around and all drank deeply.

Except the tethered boy. He was tied to one side, away from the group. He slumped forlornly on the stony ground, watching them devour the food.

"He is not one of us any more," Abdullah sneered.

Dark clouds drifted overhead, plunging the entire valley into shade. Rafiq looked around him. The steeply curving cliffs circling the valley seemed menacing, shutting him into this dark space. This was not a friendly place.

"Dig a hole," Kareem ordered abruptly.

He pointed to a flat area next to some rocks where the ground was hard and stony. The boys leaped up wordlessly. Nobody asked any questions. Kareem's mood was as dark and threatening as the sky. Rafiq took a shovel and struggled to get it into the unbreakable ground. He swung with all his might and jumped on the blade, but to no avail. It took a long time to make even a shallow depression but they persevered.

Kareem checked the depth of the hole every once in a while. "Keep digging," he repeated each time.

When it was the full depth of their shovels, he told them to stop and put their tools away. Rafiq laid down his shovel and wiped his shirtsleeve across his sweating face, watching with interest as Kareem seized the prisoner. Then, to Rafiq's astonishment, Kareem flung the boy into the hole. Rafiq blinked and looked at Kareem, whose voice was steady when he spoke, hard as the rocky ground.

"Stone him," he ordered. "He tried to betray us: his brothers, his family. He deserves to die." He spat at the boy.

"He will never make a soldier."

The boy prisoner stared at Kareem from the hole, his eyes wide with disbelief, his body stiff with shock. Rafiq stared too, feeling sickness rise in his throat. His ears started buzzing. His heart pounded so that he thought it would burst out of his chest.

"Please. No," the boy pleaded, his small voice a solo cry rising upwards in the vast silence of the mountains. "No. Please. I just want to go home."

He tried desperately to clamber out of the hole but the ropes binding his limbs stopped him. His knees tore on the stony ground. The other boys stood and watched him struggle. Nobody moved. Sweat trickled between Rafiq's shoulder blades, and his breath came in quick shallow gasps.

"Kill him," Kareem ordered again. "And any boy who does not stone him can join him in the grave."

Abdullah reached down and picked up the first stone. It hurtled through the air and hit the boy on the shoulder. He stumbled from the impact and looked up, his face shocked.

And then they started. Reluctantly at first.

Rafiq picked up a pebble and lobbed it half-heartedly into the hole, missing the boy. Even though he missed, the boy looked at him directly so that Rafiq thought his heart would break.

"Why?" he asked. "We're from the same village. We went to—"

A stone thrown by somebody else hit him on the temple. He flinched with pain, crouching down to protect his face.

Rafiq was glad that he hadn't finished his accusations, because he didn't want to listen to his words, his blame. He knew this was a terrible thing. But everything was terrible. He didn't want to fight this war. He didn't want to set mines and injure people; to dig graves and kill his schoolmates. He was ten years old and should have been in school. The choice given to him was to kill this boy or die in the stony hole next to him.

Rafiq felt tears spill from his eyes. He wanted to yell that he didn't want to die. He didn't want the boy to die either, but he had no choice. He felt angry with the boy for making him cry, for making him weak. It brought shame on his family and it was this boy's fault. He had already shamed his own family, and now he had shamed Rafiq and his brothers in the mountains.

Rafiq started to pick up rocks and fling them at the weak, shameful boy. Faster and faster. He wanted this boy to stop looking at him and asking him why.

The air was thick with stones now, getting faster and bigger and more accurate. The boys stood in a circle around the hole, so it was easier to believe that the stones that hit the boy prisoner were thrown by somebody else. Rafiq wasn't the one who hit him on the face so that his forehead opened and bled. Rafiq wasn't the one who watched him wet himself with terror and then aimed at the wet patch. Rafiq wasn't the one… Rafiq wasn't the one…

He was kneeling on the ground, sobbing and gasping, when Ahmed touched his shoulder, telling him to stop. It was over; there was no need to throw any more stones. Rafiq looked, and after a moment or two, he saw. The boy was motionless in the bottom of the hole, stones and rocks littered over his small damaged body. His face was turned downwards, his arms flung behind him, trying to shield himself. They all stood in a silent circle for a moment. Boys dropped on the ground the stones they still held in their hands.

Kareem spat on the lifeless body. "Cover it up," he told them.

Wearily they picked up their shovels once again and filled the hole. As they left the dark valley, Rafiq hung his aching head. He did not feel strong or proud that afternoon. He felt broken.

13

The cold season clawed its way steadily into the high mountains. Snow drifted from the peaks down to their valley, filling the corners and crevices. The air smelled of it days before it arrived. Frost settled on the roofs of their huts. The boys huddled together around the fire and on their mats at night, seeking warmth from each other. The ice lacing the river's edge grew thick and glossy until Rafiq could stand on it. He always waited for the chill to numb his toes, to creep into his bones. The rawness somehow made his endurance real, bore witness to the strength of his body. Only then did he bend to the task of filling his buckets as the ice creaked and cracked beneath him.

Since becoming a true Kashmiri freedom fighter, he was usually first out of his hut in the morning, waking well before the other boys. The door was left unlocked now and

Rafiq slipped out silently, a dark shadow. Whenever he was ahead of the old man, which was not often, he woke the sleeping embers to make the new fire for the day, feeding them dry kindling until they spat life at him.

Once he had completed his water runs, he stood close to the sputtering flames, drinking hot tea with the old man and Abdullah while the other boys started their duties. Abdullah talked with the old man about the missions the freedom fighters would carry out, the goals they must accomplish, and their contacts and supporters in distant places. Rafiq listened; and although much of the detailed discussion was unfamiliar, he believed that what he was hearing was important for a soldier to learn and understand.

"You should be making more use of the new boys," the old man told Abdullah one morning as Rafiq watched tiny flakes of snow swirl through the air and vanish into the steam curling from his mug.

Abdullah cleared his throat and spat on the ground. "Soon. My work with them is almost complete."

The old man nodded. "Was it worth it?"

Abdullah shrugged. "Some are good, one or two exceptional. They will take this war to a new level. In the future they will lead. They have already shown themselves to be ready for more important work."

From the corner of his eye Rafiq saw Abdullah glance in his direction and knew that the words were intended for his ears. He felt a warmth spread through his blood and it was a good feeling. His spine stretched straighter and his thoughts grew bigger because Abdullah had acknowledged his skills as a free soldier of Kashmir. From that day on he waited patiently for the time to come when Abdullah would send him on important missions.

The bitter weather continued for many weeks. Rafiq had never experienced such a dead, penetrating cold as this. It crept upwards from the ground, stiffening his muscles and dulling his thoughts so that he went around in a half-trance. They needed to eat more food to stay warm, and soon the meagre supplies had dwindled to a few sacks of rice and flour.

Abdullah spoke to them one evening. "Tomorrow a group will ride from camp to collect food from villages in the valleys. I need volunteers."

The boys stood in a knot and stared, not sure what to say.

Ahmed dug Rafiq in the ribs. "Do you want to go?" he whispered.

Rafiq was confused. They didn't get choices, only orders. He didn't know how to respond.

Ahmed continued, grinning. "It's something different. Away from camp. It'll be fun."

Rafiq was annoyed. This wasn't a place for fun. He had no time for fun. He had a war to fight for Allah. But Ahmed was already waving his hand in the air, dragging Rafiq's up by the sleeve. Abdullah counted them in and that was it. Rafiq's confusion was immediately replaced by apprehension. He didn't know what was going to happen, and experience had taught him that new things at camp were not normally good.

That night, Rafiq lay wide-eyed on his sleeping mat, shivering under his blanket, his stomach tight and his thoughts racing while other boys snored. He had heard of these trips to collect food. They kept goats at camp, so there was no shortage of meat, milk and cheese, but they weren't able to grow crops in the hostile dirt that covered the mountains. On a regular basis they raided surrounding villages or passing buses for flour, oil and vegetables, even warm clothing and shoes. But what if they raided a place he recognized? Or the ride took him somewhere that woke his buried memories? The riding frightened him too, for he had never been on a horse and he was terrified of the huge powerful animals with their sweaty hides and flaring nostrils.

In spite of his fears he was eventually overcome with exhaustion and fell asleep, although it was dreamless. He had stopped dreaming a long time ago.

The next morning, after tea and prayers, the men roped up the horses. Ahmed was excited. He came running from the stores with armfuls of old blankets to sling over the animals' backs. They stamped and snorted in the dirt, throwing up clouds of fine dust, sparkling with ice. Once the horses were loaded with guns and empty sacks, the boys mounted them. Kareem hoisted Rafiq high in the air and dumped him onto the back of a large piebald that tossed its head aggressively and cavorted around wildly no matter how hard Rafiq hauled on the reins.

Six other boys saddled up, kicking their heels and shouting at their mounts. The camp's half-wild dogs barked and snapped at the horses' hooves, further agitating them. It was all frenzied activity and noise and dust until the lead scout blasted his gun into the sky, and then they were off at a charge, hurtling over the hills and down steep slopes, ignoring the worn tracks. The horses snapped and snorted at each other as they jostled for lead position. Rafiq was petrified and clung on for his life, letting his wild charger race freely with the rest of them. Ahmed galloped past, clearly an experienced rider, and whooped with excitement as Rafiq gritted his teeth and scowled.

When the horses had expended their first rush of energy, they slowed down and dropped their heads as they picked their way over the dry barren earth. The route got steeper and narrower. A thick coating of ice lurked in the shadows and the air glittered with drifting ice crystals. Moving in single file, they carefully stepped their way around rocky outcrops and along narrow cliff paths.

Rafiq was finally able to sit upright and he gazed ahead, squinting in the low white sun. The mountains stretched for ever into the distance, ridge after ridge as far as his eye could see, until they were lost in the hazy blueness. He felt tiny.

To one side of the trail a sheer cliff face plummeted downwards. Occasionally the horses dislodged loose

boulders that cascaded into the ravine. Rafiq hea
crashing and splintering against the rock face, and
after a long silence, smashing to pieces on the valley

The group descended from the upper hills and reac̄ed
softer folds of dusty earth criss-crossed by camel tracks.

"Move with the rhythm of your horse when he gallops,"
Ahmed told Rafiq, trotting alongside. "Don't fight it."

"I think he wants to throw me off."

Ahmed laughed. "He doesn't even notice you," he said.
"It'll be easier to gallop where the land is flat."

Rafiq looked around at the familiar landscape. He recognized the rise and fall of the lower plains and felt a sadness in his heart. The lead scout let out a whoop and they
were off again, galloping over the slopes and wide spaces,
leaving broken memories behind.

Rafiq tried to follow Ahmed's advice and eventually
managed to match the rhythm of his animal's gallop. He
began to enjoy the speed. The wind tore through his hair
and his blood pounded. His horse was powerful beneath
him and Rafiq felt the heat of its back rising through the
blanket.

They reached their destination, a small village, by early
afternoon. While still some distance away, they slowed to
a trot. The scout called them together and they gathered
around.

"We haven't been here before," he told the boys. "It's
not good to raid the same settlements or we'll turn people against us. We're here for food and supplies only. No

killing or hurting anyone unless necessary. We stock up and leave. No more. Don't clean them out entirely: these are Kashmiri people. We don't wish them to go hungry; we just want them to share what they have so we can continue our fight."

The raiders pulled up their orange bandannas to cover their faces. Rafiq felt stronger with his face masked, a real soldier, and wondered if the others felt the same. They swung their AK-47s from their backs.

Spurring their half-wild horses into a fast gallop, the boys whooped and yelled, firing their guns into the sky, and raced down the dried mud track through the village, pulling up in the beaten earth area at its centre, where children queued at the village tap. Their loud entrance filled the air with pounding hooves and dust and the villagers came running to see what the commotion was about.

As the lead rider shouted the usual words about fighting for the liberation of Kashmir from the injustices and oppression of the Indian government, Rafiq looked at the faces of those gathered about. They stared in bewilderment at these masked boys on horseback, swinging their guns about. He knew how they felt. He understood their frightened, confused expressions. They eyed the guns warily and only seemed to comprehend what was happening when the boys slid off the backs of the horses and ran into their homes, emerging with armfuls of corncobs, bags of flour and cans of fuel, which they loaded onto the horses.

The villagers moved aside and let the boys take what they wanted, watching them in silence.

Rafiq burst into the nearest house. "I'm a soldier of Kashmir," he shouted into the gloom. "We are fighting the war to free our country! We need provisions to keep strong."

There was a woman squatting over a smoking fire, breastfeeding her baby. Rafiq immediately averted his eyes but the woman didn't move. She looked at him and then went back to stirring the pot on the fire. As Rafiq's eyes grew accustomed to the dim light, he saw two children in the single room. One was a toddler, naked, with a runny nose and sores around her mouth, and the second a small boy playing among a heap of clothes in the corner. Rafiq looked around but there was little to take: one small bag of meal, a few potatoes, a sack of flour. After a moment's hesitation, he scooped up the sack of flour and left.

Outside, an old man was appealing to the raiders not to take his chickens. Two of the boys had stuffed some hens into a cloth sack, which they were now tying onto a saddle-bag. They ignored the man's plaintive cries and the birds' squawking protests. The old man shuffled up to them and put his hand on one boy's shoulder.

"I sell their eggs," he told them in a cracked voice. "That's how I live. I sell the eggs from my chickens. They're all I have."

The boys finished securing the sacks and pushed past him to enter another house.

"Please," the old man begged, grasping the boy's shoulder more tightly. "Don't take my chickens."

The boy swung round, his eyes flashing. "I'm leaving two laying hens for you," he shouted in the old man's face and then jabbed him in the chest, hard, with the butt of his rifle. The old man fell in the dirt, wheezing, and the boy stepped over him.

Rafiq lowered his eyes and reminded himself sharply that he was a soldier now, not a village boy. But he spent a long time putting the single sack of flour in his saddlebag and didn't enter any more houses.

The whole raid was over in a few minutes. There was no further resistance but the hoard was not rich. It was a poor village and the boys rode away with little to show for their long ride and flamboyant display.

It was late when they reached the mountains. Darkness and bright stars made the route strange. Unseen creatures flitted in the sky or scrabbled among the stones that slowly froze together, creaking eerily, and the young raiders were relieved to see the welcome glow of the camp when they finally arrived.

It was far easier to fight a war than to raid a village, Rafiq decided.

14

Although he was always in her thoughts, Jameela didn't speak of Rafiq any more. Her father had forbidden any mention of his name after the village had learned that the stolen boys had become militants, terrorists fighting a war and killing innocent civilians. They had known for over a year now – ever since the day Jameela had seen the lone boy on the mountain road. That day, there had been wild talk about it when the bus arrived at Varahamula. A woman from their village had come running after them as they made their way through the streets to the market.

"I saw the boy too – the one your daughter saw," she said to Jameela's mother. "It was one of our stolen boys. I'm certain of it."

Another woman joined them and spoke up, her face hidden by her hijab. "I noticed him. He looked so lost, so sad… I think he's my neighbour's child. I'll speak to her when we get home."

"Did you see the other boys fleeing up the mountain?" the first woman asked. "I recognized two of them. Brothers. My sister's children. She'll tell you herself."

She called to a woman who was fumbling to put change into a little pouch. "I saw my sons," she confirmed, her eyes welling with tears. "After almost a whole year without them. And they ran from me. Ran into the mountains rather than come home on the local bus. What notions have been put into their heads? What fears have filled them so much that they flee from their own people?"

The other women comforted her. "They didn't see you. They didn't know you were on the bus. Why would they run from their own mother?"

Jameela noticed that her mother hung on to every word the women said.

"Why do you pay such attention to these women, yet when I told you, you scarcely listened?" she asked when they had moved on.

Her mother smiled at her indignant daughter. "Because you're too like me, Jameela. You see what your mind dreams of and hopes for. I know you saw a boy up in the mountains, but your wish to see Rafiq is as strong as mine, and I thought perhaps your dreams had put the face of a village child on that boy."

"But I know what I saw, Mamma. It was not my dreams," Jameela said earnestly.

"I know that, child," her mother replied. "Later today we'll report what you saw to the authorities. The other women will come too and we will ask the police to do something. It has been too long and no news coming."

They went to the police station that afternoon, opposite the beautiful White Mosque. There were other men and women there, clamouring to tell the authorities what they had seen. But the police had shocking news for them, of fresh explosions on the mountain road in the exact spot where the bus had braked and the boys had been seen.

"Those were not village children you saw," the police told them.

"But they were," the villagers insisted. "We saw our own children. With our own eyes."

"Then they have joined up with Kashmiri militants. Your boys have become terrorists. Setting mines and killing people. Ambushing officials and murdering them. They are not your true sons any more."

The police then told them that a bus carrying pilgrims to a holy festival in a distant village had been blown up in the explosions, men and women killed and injured. The authorities said the mines had only been set that morning, and they were very interested in what the village people had to tell them. They took detailed descriptions and asked numerous questions. How many boys? How many men? What ages? Where did they run to? The villagers said that they might have seen guns. There was mention of sticks and shovels, strange behaviour and fleeing as soon as the bus stopped.

Except for that one lonely little boy, left all on his own on the road.

When Jameela's father heard the news and took in all that his wife and daughter had to tell him after their eventful trip, he fell silent and did not speak about it. But later that evening Jameela noticed him alone in the courtyard, scanning the distant peaks of the Pir Panjals, tracing their jagged contours. And from that day on, his shoulders seemed to slump a little lower and his eyes seemed to be more interested in studying the ground, as if it were too difficult for him to raise them any higher.

Several days later, as they shared their evening meal, their father spoke softly, his voice cracking so he had to stop and clear his throat before starting again.

"My lost son is no longer a child of this home," he began. "Mahmood is now my firstborn son and will be so from this day on."

Jameela felt her heart breaking. She looked at her mother, who was sitting in silence, her hands folded in her lap, gazing down at her meal. A single tear ran down her face. Mahmood was staring at his father in astonishment, but, for once, was wise enough to say nothing.

"The village has mourned the loss of its sons," their father continued. "We have prayed and grieved for our own great loss." He paused and swallowed. "But he is gone from our lives now. There will be no more talk of our lost son. He is no longer of this family."

Jameela felt the sadness of the universe settle in her

bones when she realized that her father could not even speak Rafiq's name.

Not everyone in the village felt as strongly as her father. Jameela talked to her friends about it as they filled the water jars at the village tap.

"My father wants my two brothers to come home again," said one. "It doesn't matter what they have done. He just wants them back."

"My papa said he will beat Mohammed when he comes home and send him to live with the goats," another friend added, "because of what he has done to other people. But my mother said that she will protect him and take care of him. She calls him her baby even though he's now twelve."

Jameela also spoke to her mother, but only when her father was away from the house. "What Papa says is wrong, Mamma," she said, passion flooding into her voice.

"Hush, Jameela," her mother replied sharply. "Don't ever speak that way about your father. He is a good man."

Jameela's eyes filled with tears, for she loved her father yet could not agree with his decision regarding Rafiq.

"Rafiq did not want to go away," she continued, carefully softening her voice to avoid further angering her mother, who was kneading bread as though her life depended on it. "He is a good boy, Mamma. Papa taught him to be kind. It's the bad men in the mountains making him do these things. He is my brother and he's not bad."

But her mother tightened her lips and refused to look at her daughter. Clouds of flour puffed up from the soft dough as she punched it. Jameela went to her and put her hand over her mother's floury one. Her mother paused in her work, but her head stayed down.

"We can't forget Rafiq, Mamma. And we can't let Papa forget him either."

Her mother jerked her head up and Jameela was surprised to see tears spilling down her cheeks.

"And what else can we do, Jameela? We must respect your papa. He is the head of this house and, unless Rafiq returns to us, you will do as your father says."

She went back to her kneading. There was no further discussion. And although Jameela longed to tell her father how she felt, to try to make him understand, she knew it wasn't her place to do this.

The seasons passed and Rafiq's name was never mentioned. Her father kept his word and Mahmood became his favoured son. Even when her father was at the mosque with Mahmood, Jameela did not mention Rafiq to her mother or to Afrah.

But with Imraan it was different. With Imraan she brought Rafiq alive through her stories. As the youngest, Imraan had no memory of his older brother; to him Mahmood had always been the oldest boy, and if it weren't for Jameela he would have known nothing of Rafiq. Sometimes when she tucked Imraan into his cot at night,

Jameela told him stories of a brave and loving brother of whom he should be very proud.

"These are secret stories only for you, Imraan. No one else will hear them and you must tell nobody."

Imraan would nod at her, wide-eyed, listening to every word of the colourful, exciting tales of Rafiq. The magical stories that Jameela shared only with him made him feel important, because now he knew some of the best things about Rafiq – and they were his to treasure.

"When your big brother was only six years old, he climbed from the flat roof of this house all the way down the walnut tree to the ground because I had forgotten to shut the door of the henhouse before going to bed," Jameela told him, her eyes shining with the warmth of the memory. "Rats or foxes could creep in at night and steal the baby chickens, and Papa would beat me black and blue for such carelessness. You see, it was my job to shut the hens in and it was silly of me to forget. Rafiq put his arm round my shoulder because I was trembling, Imraan. Later in the night, when the whole house was asleep, he climbed onto the roof and swung across to the walnut tree. He shut the henhouse door and climbed back up again. The hens were safe and Rafiq never told."

And with tears sparkling in her eyes, she told Imraan how Rafiq had taught her to read from his school books, hunkering down with her in the courtyard, the books spread open on their laps. He had shown her how the language was formed on the page and how the beautiful rhythm of the words rose and fell with the curves and swirls of the letters. Jameela had loved learning from him, tracing the shapes with her finger, repeating the words after Rafiq. None of her friends' brothers had taught reading to their sisters, so Jameela had always thought herself blessed to have a brother like Rafiq.

15

The stick cracked across the soles of his bare feet. Rafiq recoiled and was instantly awake, jerking upright on the seat of the jeep. Kareem reached down and poked the small boy curled up on the floor behind the driver's seat. Ten-year-old Samir yelped and sleepily pushed the stick away. Rafiq, a teenager and almost a man, jumped out.

"It's very warm," Samir commented as he sat up and looked towards the distant Pir Panjals. "There's no breeze and the air is dead and heavy."

"We need water," Rafiq told him.

Samir had never been out of the mountains before and everything was new to him. The Pir Panjals were hazy in the cool morning air and very far away. "Look how small the mountains have become," he remarked, his voice full of wonder.

"Samir!" Rafiq's voice was sharp.

Samir leaped over the side of the jeep and ran to him.

"Fetch the water." Rafiq handed the boy a container and pointed. "There's a stream over there."

Samir ran off. While they waited for him to return, Kareem set a fire and Rafiq cleared the branches that had been placed to conceal the jeep's presence. During prayers Rafiq asked for success in their mission. It would be difficult and he was particularly worried about Samir, who was giddy and lacked concentration. Afterwards they boiled up tea and sugar. The steam swirled in the still air as they drank the hot brew, squatting around the fire.

"Time to leave," Kareem said.

He tinkered with the jeep's ignition before the old vehicle spluttered and got started. Samir scooped handfuls of sand over the fire and they were off, bumping and jerking over rough ground until they reached the dirt track.

"Look at all the trees and bushes," Samir remarked. "Have you ever seen so many in one place?"

It was several hours before they joined up with the surfaced road. Kareem swung the jeep towards the town of Poonch. The potholed strip of tarmac snaked through the countryside, passing smallholdings and villages.

Little children stood on the roadside and watched the jeep pass. Apart from Samir's frequent observations about everything, there was no conversation. Rafiq concentrated on the assignment and everyone's role in it. Kareem concentrated on getting there and getting the business done.

Samir concentrated on all he saw. It was a long day of driving.

They stopped twice: once to relieve themselves in the bushes; and a second time at a little stall on the roadside where the proprietor served them meals of rice and dhal on metal trays with chutney and curd.

"This food is so different from home," Samir announced. "Fit for a king. Look at the peach chutney! And sweet fresh curd!"

They sat on wooden benches set to one side of the stall and left fifteen minutes later. Kareem paid with grubby notes. The stallholder watched them leave, scratching his armpit as they drove off.

The white heat had burnt out of the sun and the light had sweated itself to a softer shade by the time they reached the outskirts of the main town. Shanty dwellings of cardboard and plastic sheeting appeared on each side of the road. There were ragged children hanging around at the traffic intersections, begging from the drivers. Stray dogs wandered everywhere. Skinny cows stood chewing bits of old cardboard. Kareem constantly blared the horn and swerved around the obstacles, muttering angrily.

"This is what has been done to my people," he commented sourly, breaking his silence. "We have no pride left. We are tyrannized by the Indian government."

Rafiq stared around him and couldn't remember when he had last seen so many people. Women squatted in little huddles in the dirt, babies clinging to them. There were men too, asleep on the roadside or sitting on walls. Cycle rickshaws, pedalled by old men or young boys, squeezed through the teeming traffic, their bells ringing loudly.

Kareem had to keep braking to avoid cars and vans, rickshaws and buses, children and dogs. He sweated, continually wiping his hands on his black beard. He was out of place and uncomfortable in this town.

Huge buses crammed high with bags and passengers, some sitting on the roof, passed them, religious songs blaring from the sound systems, diesel fumes filling the air with a hot choking smell. They drove past a market swarming with local people shopping and haggling, their voices raised as they argued and bartered.

Rafiq's head buzzed, while beside him Samir stared at everything, struck silent. Every sense was assaulted by something new and he was dizzy with looking. As the child of a mountain tribe, his world comprised the brown rolling mountains with their winter snows and scalding summer heat, small herds of goats and sheep, and a handful of families eking out a survival in the austere surroundings.

"There should be a deserted area of land after this roundabout. I need to turn left at it."

Kareem's voice was cracking with impatience. Samir and Rafiq immediately sat up, searching for empty plots.

"There's a new building there." Rafiq pointed to where rickety scaffolding clung precariously to a fresh concrete structure, crawling with local workers clambering up and down ladders. "Maybe that's where the site was."

Kareem looked at the building and then in his mirror. After a lot of swerving and braking he swung off the main road and headed down side streets. He made a couple of aggressive turns and one reverse where Samir was ordered into the road to direct the jeep. Eventually he turned the vehicle into quieter streets. There was little traffic here. The noise of the frenzy faded behind them as Kareem drove down ever-narrower alleys. He finally stopped at the door of a small house tucked between a shop and a boarded-up building.

"How do people live in such small spaces?" Samir piped up, having recovered his powers of speech.

The small jeep blocked the whole street. Kareem climbed out, took a long stretch and farted. "Get out," he ordered Rafiq; and to Samir: "You stay here."

Samir squatted on the seat and looked out. There was enough to keep him occupied for the next six months. Kareem knocked on the door.

As they waited, Rafiq became aware of someone watching them. Wary of being caught by the authorities, he turned quickly to see, but it was only a child, a small girl with dark eyes who peeked from the open doorway of the house opposite. She smiled shyly at him, but shrank into the doorway when he didn't smile back. Her big eyes and glossy hair reminded him briefly of somebody, but he couldn't be certain. He felt a sudden sadness, but the memory slipped from his mind; and abruptly this child he was gazing at was just a stranger and he was a soldier again, preparing for a mission.

Annoyed with himself, he ignored her and turned back as locks slid open on the inside of the door. It opened a crack.

"Yes?"

"I am here with my children seeking a room for the night," Kareem replied.

"How many children have you?"

"I have two boys of ten and fourteen. We have travelled far and are very tired."

"Where is the mother of your children?"

"She is sick and needs treatment. We have come to town to buy medicine for her."

There was a pause and then the door was opened.

"We have room for you and your sons."

Rafiq and Kareem were admitted to the safe house and the door shut behind them. The women in the house disappeared, only emerging again to serve glasses of hot mint tea and dishes of rice and eggs, aubergines and tomatoes to their guests, who ate with the men sitting on the floor of an upstairs room. Once eating was over, the men got down to business. Tomorrow was the day of their mission and there was planning to do.

First they had to unload the jeep.

Under cover of darkness they carried in boxes of explosives, detonators and wiring, wrapped in heavy plastic. When the jeep was empty, Samir came in also, glad to be out of the dark street. As he was too young and inexperienced to be involved in the detailed planning, he ate his food then stretched himself on the floor and slept while Rafiq and the older men continued their discussions. They studied plans of the centre of the town, locating landmarks and marketplaces, temples and main roads. They discussed tactics and approaches, escape routes and safe hiding places. They opened up the boxes of weapons and sorted through what was needed, checking that it was all in good condition and ready to use.

When Rafiq finally lay down to rest much later that night, he found his sleep more fractured than usual. The noises of the town were alien to him and disturbed his slumber. He started as car horns blared. Voices carried far in the night air. Dogs barked. Vehicles revved their engines and backfired. There were unfamiliar smells also, smells of which Rafiq was normally unaware: rotting vegetables discarded on the street, open sewers and stinking corners where people relieved themselves, car and lorry fumes, all mingling together in the hot air. These were absent in the mountains, where brisk breezes whipped away any odours.

He had visions too. Whenever he closed his eyes, the image of a child appeared, a small girl with dark hair and a gentle smile and Rafiq sensed a warmth in him he had not known for a long time. He kept his eyes shut tightly so that her image would stay with him, but then the sun was shining in his eyes, dazzling him, and it was morning.

"Get up, Rafiq. It's time to go."

Samir was shaking him by the shoulder and Rafiq woke

and was embarrassed to see the others already up and getting ready to leave. He gobbled the flatbread and chickpeas brought by the women, then they left the safe house, heading for the main chowk.

Rafiq took note of their route, frequently looking back to confirm twists in the alleys and distinctive shopfronts. There was no breeze in the winding narrow streets, and although it was early the heat built up fast. Cars and vans queued impatiently in single file, edging their way slowly forward, constantly blasting their horns as they squeezed past. As the trio drew closer to the centre of the town, the hot lanes and alleys filled with more people. Rafiq looked at them, wondering where so many people could be going at this time of morning.

"Where could so many people be going at this time of morning?" Samir asked.

Rafiq felt uncomfortable in the pressing crowds and pushed back at the bodies crowding in on him. They reached the wide and sunny chowk, where stalls were set up, selling all manner of goods. Hawkers stood on street corners and shouted loudly, touting their wares to passers-by.

"Chai, chai, chai," yelled a chai wallah, selling little pottery cups of sweet tea with ginger and cardamom. Rafiq stumbled with fright when he shouted almost in his face, and bumped into Kareem. Kareem pushed back, irritated, himself a little dizzy with all the activity although he was a grown man with experience of towns.

Next to the chai wallah, a tiny shrivelled woman was

frying vegetable samosas in a vat of bubbling oil. She served them smoking hot, in a fold of torn newspaper. Something about their aroma woke a memory deep in Rafiq's head and he stopped in his tracks, caught in an unexpected web of familiarity. Images of village streets and dusty classrooms flitted through his thoughts, distracting him.

"We must go," Kareem said sharply and strode off across the square.

Rafiq snapped out of his reverie and tore after him. They had business to do. This morning's work was to check out the locations and access points they had identified on the plans.

"Turn right here." Kareem pointed to the street name. "This corner is important. Take note of it."

Once they turned, the streets became narrow and twisted again angling sharply in different directions. Eventually they reached the cloth bazaar. Masses of stalls were crammed into a small open area, heaped with hanks of wool and cloth, spools of threads and cones of yarns. Tall poles overhead fluttered with stitched shirts and shalwars, while tailors and merchants hovered around their stalls, entreating passers-by to view their goods.

Kareem, Rafiq and Samir walked through slowly, looking for one particular stall on the corner of one particular street.

"Here it is," Samir cried suddenly, pointing up at the street name, proud that he was able to make out the words. "This is what we've been looking for."

Below it was an untidy stall, its wooden counter stacked with loose heaps of cloth and rolls of fabric.

"Can I help?" asked the owner, lurking in the dark recesses of a shop at the rear. He shuffled out, wringing his hands, and peered curiously at the small boy from beneath shaggy eyebrows.

Kareem stepped forward, blocking Samir. "I understand that this alley leads directly to the temple?" he enquired.

The owner shifted his gaze and smiled at Kareem. "You can follow it all the way there. It twists and turns like a stuck snake. Don't take any side lanes and you will arrive in less than ten minutes."

The trio moved off. Once they were out of view, Rafiq reached out and cuffed Samir hard on the back of the head.

"Never draw attention to yourself in that way. You may be identified later on."

Samir stumbled from the blow and hung his head. He nodded and kept walking, his eyes downcast.

Rafiq turned to Kareem. "It's perfect for our needs."

Kareem nodded. "Right at the mouth of this alley so you will immediately be protected from the blast." His lip curled in a sneer. "And a lazy Indian shopkeeper who leaves his stall unattended."

In a matter of minutes, they arrived at the temple. It was a very important one, visited daily by large numbers of worshippers. Even at this early hour, pilgrims from across the country were visiting the shrines and making devotions to their gods and goddesses. The air was thick with incense and candle smoke.

"These people worship false deities," Kareem told the boys. "They are our enemies. The brothers and sisters of India. Not true Kashmiris. You need to understand why this iniquity must be destroyed. Come!"

They climbed the steps to the temple entrance and took off their sandals, which they left outside among the pile of pilgrims' shoes. Samir trotted after Kareem, gazing around in wonder, but Rafiq hesitated in the portico.

"Is it right that we enter?" he asked. Kareem paused and stared at him. Rafiq blushed, but continued. "Why anger Allah by entering a temple to other gods?"

"We are doing it *for* Allah," Kareem stated. "It is necessary so we can plan for our mission."

He turned and went in, leaving Rafiq standing alone. The boy considered Kareem's words. He reasoned with himself that if he didn't go in, he would not be able to carry out this mission properly. And his mission was for God. He murmured some supplications, seeking protection and forgiveness, and then entered.

The atmosphere was thick with sweet smells that hung in the air, making everything gauzy. Fat waxy candles smoked and dripped in front of painted images of fierce-looking deities. Rafiq walked slowly from one mural to the next, not understanding how people could revere such meaningless images. He gazed around as men and women worshipped the idols and knelt in submission to huge gold and silver statues and effigies. No one noticed his candid staring, so totally absorbed were they in their prayers.

Rafiq was shocked to see clean-shaven men and bare-headed women mixing openly in the areas of worship, their eyes shut and their faces serene. He had never seen anything like this before and was astonished by the lack of modesty. Some of the women carried babies with eyes blackened with kohl and ears hung with hoops of gold and silver.

Kareem came and spoke in his ear. "We need to see the back of this building."

Rafiq nodded and trailed after him. It was essential that Kashmir cleanse itself of these infidels, he thought. His faith was clean and pure, without all the trappings and frippery he had witnessed in the temple. Slipping on his sandals, he ran after Kareem and Samir to view the escape routes available to them at the rear.

By the time the sun was high, they had gathered all the information they required. It was time to go back to the safe house, to pray for success and to ready themselves.

16

Samir was fascinated by the mirror.

It hung on the wall of the room in which the two boys were preparing their equipment. He stroked its cool surface with his dirty fingers. He had never seen one before and was mesmerized by his own never-seen reflection, pulling foolish faces at himself until Rafiq noticed and reprimanded him for his behaviour.

"Come away. This is no time for childish games," he told him severely. "You are a soldier fighting a war. Don't behave like those pilgrims we saw earlier. Our people are not taken in by foolish worldly goods."

Rafiq was solemn and tightly focused now they were close to their time, but Samir was even more flighty than usual. Rafiq had known this was going to happen. He'd warned Kareem and Abdullah about Samir long ago but they wouldn't listen, because they wanted a young child

147

who would not attract attention for this mission. But diminutive size seemed to be Samir's only asset. He had been distracted throughout the journey to Poonch; he had shown lack of discipline in the cloth bazaar; and now he was more interested in his own foolish expressions than their critical mission for freedom. Rafiq's blood heated as he stood over the child. He clenched his fists, muttering to calm his breathing, and lifted a heavy leather belt.

"Put this on and tighten it," he ordered.

The child looped the belt around his small waist and pulled the heavy strap. It was soft and flexible and yielded easily to his tough little hands. Kareem had had to punch many extra holes in the ammunition belt to fit the small bodies to which it had been strapped over the years. Just to be sure, Rafiq ran an extra strap across Samir's bare chest and over one shoulder.

"Is it secure?"

Samir nodded.

"Check the clips and pins on every grenade," Rafiq ordered, handing over the box of grenades and watching as Samir knelt down and began his task. Rafiq saw the child's fingers tremble as he worked and was satisfied that his presence was sharpening his concentration. Rafiq squatted down next to him and continued cleaning his gun, keeping a close eye on Samir as he attached each grenade to his belt.

Kareem was in the yard, mixing the components needed to make incendiary devices. He returned moments later carrying a plastic bag bulging with them. The powerful handmade explosives were each wrapped in newspaper tied with twine. They looked as if they could be packets of anything: sugar, rice, medicines, which should deter any curious individuals who might by chance notice a small boy placing them at various locations around the temple. But small skinny boys wandering around were never noticed, much less watched, and there was little likelihood of Samir being stopped or questioned.

"What are you to say if anyone sees you leaving these packages around?" Kareem demanded as he carefully put the bag down.

Samir looked up from the floor. "Oh, thank you—" he began.

"Do it properly," Rafiq said, nudging him sharply with his foot.

Samir jumped to his feet and faced Kareem. He started again.

"Oh, thank you. That is the medicine for my sick mamma that I have just collected. I came into the temple to pray for her and now I nearly leave her medicine behind. Thank you, thank you."

His grave face suddenly lit up with a wide innocent smile as he stretched out both hands to graciously accept the package Kareem held out to him. Rafiq and Kareem nodded as the fake smile dropped from Samir's face.

Once safely in place around the temple, the bombs would be detonated by gunfire. Samir liked that part the best. The explosions were the most exciting bit.

"Get dressed," Kareem told him, "then we will pray for the success of our mission."

It was mid-afternoon. The temple was crowded and hot. It hummed with the hushed voices of praying pilgrims who shuffled around lighting candles and incense. Flower petals were strewn over the polished feet of the effigies and fluttered on the rising currents of heated air.

Rafiq and Samir strolled casually up the marble steps leading to the main shrine; Rafiq's arm rested affectionately on Samir's shoulders, but this was only to mislead any onlookers. His thoughts were completely focused on his assignment. He carried a paper-wrapped parcel in the crook of his elbow and a plastic carrier bag which he held slightly away from his body as if it might contain a dozen fresh eggs. They didn't speak to each other, but paused together on the steps and looked into the interior. Rafiq handed Samir the carrier bag and turned to go back down the steps, glancing briefly to where Samir had hunkered down.

"Stay here until you see me with Kareem and have heard the explosion and the police sirens," he hissed in his ear.

Samir gazed, mesmerized, at the bustling chowk and nodded his head, but it wasn't enough assurance for Rafiq. He placed his hand threateningly on his belt, where Samir knew his knife was secreted, and loomed darkly over him, his voice menacing and low.

"Stay alert and watchful, is that clear? This mission will not fail because of your foolishness. You are no longer a boy: you are a soldier of Allah."

Samir blinked and looked up at him. "I won't let you down," he whispered.

Rafiq paused for a second, then whirled round and strode across the chowk towards the cloth bazaar, looking neither right nor left. His thoughts raced, razor sharp, filled with the precise order of how the plan would unfurl. He didn't see the people around him – parents and children, mothers with babies – strolling or hurrying through the streets, laughing and talking together. Rafiq pushed his way through them, thinking only of getting back, once the decoy was detonated, to enable the next stage to proceed.

Kareem watched from a distance, concealed behind fruit stalls at the edge of the chowk. He did not wish to be seen, because he would be remembered by onlookers. It was better that the boys should do their work alone. He would enter the action when necessary. He clutched a coarse goatskin sack, rolled and packed tightly. It was tied at the top with a strip of sinew and contained three AK-47 rifles and a bag of grenades.

Rafiq arrived at the cloth bazaar and made his way directly to the stall they had identified earlier. A group of giddy girls took up the whole front of the stall, pulling out rolls of finely woven fabrics in bright colours. The hand-wringing owner was out of his hiding place, fussing and bobbing around his customers, and the girls twittered and skittered as brilliant silks cascaded onto the table. Irritated by this intrusion into his plan, Rafiq played for time by turning his attention to the adjacent stall and fingering rolls of cotton cloth. The sharp-eyed stallholder immediately noticed him and sidled out to where he stood.

"You need a new shirt? Maybe a new shalwar?"

He smiled down at Rafiq's worn trousers and indicated the new clothing on his stall. Rafiq curled his fingers around the lethal package held close to his body.

"Thank you, no," he told the stallholder. "Not today."

"But you would like to look? My clothes will make your eyes very happy. See!"

He lifted a wooden pole and unhooked a rack of shirts from where they were suspended up high. Unexpectedly Rafiq found himself presented with more than a dozen cotton shirts. The stallholder started unbuttoning the first on the rack, showing him its fine stitching. Rafiq felt conspicuous with the attention. He did not want the stallholder to remember him. He wished to move away but the girls were still fluttering around the silk stall and the first merchant was now opening up yet more plastic-wrapped rolls of fabric.

Rafiq backed away and wandered further down the bazaar, all the time keeping a close eye on the target stall. Within moments the gaggle of girls had moved on to another stall and the disappointed stallholder disappeared into the dark recesses of his shop.

There could be no further delay.

Rafiq made his move. He quickly slipped back to the stall. He squinted into the dim shop but the merchant had his back to the counter. Rafiq glanced around furtively, confirming the proximity of the adjacent exit route down the twisting lane. He carefully swept back the folds of his shirt, revealing the incendiary device wrapped in paper, appearing no more lethal than a chicken carcass wrapped by the butcher. Poking among the folds of newspaper, Rafiq twisted the crude counter device on its side.

Thirty seconds.

That was how long he had to get away before the mechanism triggered and blasted skywards, blowing up everything within fifty metres. He plunged it deeply into the glossy folds of silk on the stall, scooping material over it until it disappeared from view. As he withdrew his hand to flee, a bony claw gripped his wrist.

Rafiq froze.

"You have come back to bargain for a shirt?" It was the astute merchant from the stall opposite. He wasn't about to lose a possible sale. Dropping his voice, he whispered conspiratorially, "I can give you a good price. Better than this stall. We can make a good deal together."

He smiled at Rafiq, pulling him towards his display.

Twenty seconds.

"No!" Rafiq raised his voice, jerking his arm, but the merchant maintained his tight grip. "I don't want your shirts."

This wasn't the way to refuse a sale, but Rafiq had no

time to observe custom. This man would soon be dead and Rafiq was not about to die with him.

The merchant released his arm and looked hard into Rafiq's eyes, then spat on the ground in disgust and withdrew to perch again on the stool at the back of his stall.

Ten seconds.

Rafiq strode fast down the lane, merging into the crowd, which surged in all directions. The alley angled abruptly to the left so that he was instantly protected from the imminent blast by tall buildings. But he was later than he should have been; he should have been further away by now.

Five seconds.

He started to sprint, knocking people aside as he took the corners of the alley.

Three seconds. Two. One.

A massive blast thundered behind him. The air shuddered; the sunlight vibrated. A deep shadow convulsed down the lane, carrying foul air and choking dust, blasting Rafiq's body along. Pain knifed through his ears and he stumbled in agony, confused and faint, colliding with a wall. The ground lurched beneath him and his stomach heaved as he tried to run, but he only succeeded in staggering a few steps before he tumbled to the dirt. All around him people ran for shelter, clutching their heads and screaming. Heavy objects thumped downwards, splintered glass sliced through the air, and shattered wooden stalls crashed to the ground.

Rafiq struggled to his knees. He had to get out of there;

had to get to the temple; had to check on Samir. Stunned, he laboured to his feet and lurched forward. He shook his head violently, trying to clear the fog that had lodged in his brain. One of his ears oozed a trickle of blood. Slowly the ground stopped heaving and settled into a gentle rocking movement. His feet found themselves again and he faltered on, his dizziness clearing, his thoughts recovering. By the time he reached the chowk, he was able to run.

With a surge of relief he saw that Samir was still in position, watching for him. He lifted his hand, signalling to the boy as he crossed to where Kareem stood coolly studying the crowds of panicked people fleeing the cloth bazaar.

Samir returned the gesture as police sirens started to wail. He was eager to get going, and now that he had spotted Rafiq he knew his time had come. He ran eagerly into the temple and rapidly placed his packages. Nobody gave him a second glance. People were caught up in the news of the explosion in the bazaar, and those fleeing the attack flooded into the temple, away from the danger.

Samir pushed his way through throngs of people, excitement filling his body as he emptied his bag of incendiaries for the foreign gods. He ran then and signalled to the others, who were already sprinting across the sun-baked chowk. Their bandannas were up, flashing bright orange, and they prised the guns from the sack as they ran. There was no need to conceal the weapons any longer. The attack was under way.

Kareem and Rafiq leaped up the steps to meet Samir, who now had his own bandanna in place and was unclipping the first of his grenades. The screams of panic started before they even reached the top step.

The three of them stormed into the temple. They discharged their weapons blindly, pumping bullets into terrified pilgrims and hurling grenades into flaming voids. Samir's incendiary devices detonated instantly, exploding into balls of flame that scorched and blackened everything within reach. The sacred spaces that had been filled with fragrant incense and the hushed cadences of prayer now vibrated with tearing cracks that brought wreckage crashing to the ground. Bitter smoke billowed, choking everyone.

The attackers blasted their guns at anybody seen running or praying, issuing chattering bursts of fire that made people convulse and spasm upwards, until they fell, twisted and twitching, to the floor.

Rafiq was aware for a moment of Samir's weapon bucking uncontrollably in his small arms as he fired wildly, its muzzle climbing to the heavens, where the bullets shot uselessly skywards as the ten-year-old struggled to wrestle it down again. And as the home-made bombs detonated, Samir whooped with a child's delight that his toys were working.

Kareem's call for retreat was scarcely audible above the chaos: he had to shout twice before Rafiq heard through the ringing in his damaged ears; then the two boys began backing towards the rear exit. Every corner of the temple was shattered or scorched. Bodies littered the floor and fires blazed, consuming the ancient frescoes, splintering the mosaics.

As they withdrew, they saw the first vehicles of the security forces tearing across the now deserted chowk, having been re-routed from the initial decoy in the cloth bazaar. Kareem blasted their way through the wooden gates at the rear of the temple with a grenade and the three of them sprinted down the narrow streets, zigzagging as the alleyways twisted and intersected endlessly, all seemingly alike.

The streets were deserted. The crackling of fires and screams of the dying faded, so that all Rafiq could hear was his own gasping breath, hammering heart and racing feet. Still they kept running, suddenly uncertain of where they were and what direction they should be going in. Kareem had parked the jeep earlier, ready for their escape, and the streets had seemed easy to follow when they had traced over the route by foot. Now they had no idea where it was.

Kareem stopped, his face dripping with sweat, his shirt stuck to his body.

"Separate," he panted. "More chance of escape. Meet at the jeep at nightfall."

"If we can find it," Rafiq muttered grimly.

They departed down different side streets, moving rapidly away from each other, concealing their guns in the folds of their clothing.

Rafiq's ears throbbed. The blood had caked down one side of his face and he scratched at it irritably. He kept stopping every few strides, straining to listen. His hearing hadn't recovered and he felt vulnerable and exposed. He wanted to cough the smoke from his lungs but was afraid to make a noise and tried to swallow the urge, his chest bursting with the effort. At one point he heard spurts of gunfire, followed by the sound of running feet. He crouched beneath a low archway and hardly breathed, although there was a rising panic in his chest that threatened to engulf him. Several times sirens sounded, but they grew distant. He heard running feet again in a parallel alley.

Gradually the light softened and the dim little streets grew as dark as Rafiq's soul. His hammering heart slowed, but his ears twitched with pain and his fingers danced on the trigger of his gun. He stayed in the stinking back alleys among the rubbish heaps, where the rats were running. He saw no one.

The stars had risen when he finally located the jeep. Kareem was skulking in a dark corner near by, his face a pale disc floating in the blackness of his hiding place.

"I saw nobody, but I heard a lot," Rafiq told him.

"I thought you or Samir had been shot," Kareem said.

"Not me," Rafiq replied. "Maybe the boy. He's not experienced enough to avoid them."

Kareem nodded.

They waited for Samir, crouching in the shadows, cocking their guns sharply at any noise. Eventually the lights in the windows of the houses were extinguished. Car engines ceased and no sirens blared. Dogs stopped barking at the stars. The smells of cooking faded and the streets were swallowed by the stillness of deep night.

The moon was high in the sky when they left the town and drove quietly towards the mountain roads. The child had not returned. As they drove back to the camp, Rafiq prayed and felt proud for him – a ten-year-old holy martyr.

17

The dust storm blew in from the west overnight: great gusts of hot wind that swept away the still air and scoured everything with sharp grits of sand and shards of dried grass. Down on the river plains, its route was hindered by villages and clumps of trees, by dips and furrows in the land, so that it was forced to slow a little. Instead it put its energy into howling unexpectedly round corners and whipping up mini-tornadoes that whirled skywards, blocking the bright stars and turning the air eerie white.

Jameela lay in her bed and listened to the storm shrieking outside her home. The mud brick walls were solid and safe, although she could hear whistling in the roof. Outside in the yard, loose objects flailed around, banging and clattering in the night. Jameela worried about her chicks. They had only hatched three days previously and she hoped the broody hen had the sense to keep them snug in the wooden henhouse.

Afrah was curled up next to Jameela, sound asleep. Although it was night-time, the light in the room shifted from silver white when the moon was clear and bright to an ethereal glow when the dust clouds stacked high and whirled in the street. Jameela watched the changing light and wished Afrah were awake to see its magic. When she was little, Afrah would awaken, trembling at the slightest storm, and she and Mahmood would cuddle up to Jameela for protection. Jameela would distract them by telling them old tales of how the spirits of the land were at war with the spirits of the sky over who would marry the water.

The land wanted to have the water living free, flowing down the mountainsides and across the valleys. The sky wanted the water to be close and protected, safe in the bright air and warmed by the sun. But the water was a clever woman and knew how to keep them both happy. She hid during their fights, letting the land and the sky battle it out. The dry wind sent from the sky would scream across the land, scouring it; the land would put up barriers to hinder the flow of the sky's anger, tripping up the wind.

When they had vented their rage at each other, the water would creep out of her hiding place and return to the soft clouds, where the sky was happy to see her; but she would tell the sky how sad she was at all the fighting. She would grieve because she wanted peace between the sky and the land, for she loved them both. Her tears would fall as soft rain so that the dry riverbeds filled with water, and the land was happy again.

And for a while, she would stay with the land, happy to run free and unhindered. But she would miss the comfort of the sky with its warm golden sun. And so, little by little, carefully and gently so as not to hurt the land, she would creep back to the sky, disguised as a dawn mist. The land never noticed her going, until one morning, she would be gone and the land would be dry again, but the sky was happy.

Up in the mountains the battle between the land and the sky raged on. The storm's fury was unhindered by obstacles and it screamed its way to a frightening crescendo, gathering up a collection of debris in its breast: missiles of bushes and bits of charcoal, armfuls of tiny pebbles and stray twigs, all of which were flung with malice at anything that got in the way.

At the militants' camp, breaths of storm wriggled under the edges of the corrugated roofs of the huts and fingered them upwards, bending over the flimsy material and sending in choking puffs of sand and dust that settled quietly on every surface. Rafiq and the other boys lay and listened to the fury as it howled over the mountain tops and slammed against their shelters. They pulled their blankets over their heads and fine dust heaped softly in the folds and pleats of wool.

Outside, there was shouting and banging as men rushed around in the wrath of the stormy night. Abdullah was fretting about the safety of the communications hut, which was the most heavily guarded and important of all the structures at the camp. There was delicate equipment in there: radios and video cameras, electronic devices and computers obtained through foreign connections at great expense. It was essential equipment for intelligence and broadcasting, and had to be protected at all costs.

The night had turned over by the time the storm reached its height. Someone hammered on the door of Rafiq's hut. It was Ahmed.

"Rafiq, get up."

He was already awake. He pushed back his blanket and wrenched open the door. Struggling out, he pulled it closed behind him. He had to plant his feet firmly and heft his full weight against the strength of the wind. Ahmed waited, his head and face wrapped in a scarf to afford him some protection. He was bent over, leaning into the wind to keep his balance, his hand clutching the scarf to prevent it being whipped across the hills.

"What's happening?" Rafiq had to shout right into his ear to be heard above the shrieking weather.

"We have to reinforce the communications hut." Ahmed's voice was barely audible although he was yelling. "The equipment will be damaged by sand. We must tie plastic sheeting over the apparatus. They are putting extra roofing on. We have to get materials from the stores."

The two boys laboured across the compound. Rafiq squinted against the wind, shielding his eyes with his hand. His teeth crunched on sand. It crept through his hair and itched his scalp. They reached the store cabin and fought to slide the heavy bolt. Inside the small shelter, dust whorled whitely in the air and eddied in the corners, but the boys were out of the bite of the storm. Rafiq coughed and spat, clearing the grit from his throat. The warm air inside was full of the smell of the cabin's contents mingled together incongruously – sweet oranges and engine oil, cinnamon and rubber hosing.

"Plastic sheeting and rope," Ahmed muttered, scrabbling through stacked sacks of foodstuffs, crates and boxes of equipment. It was as dark as sin.

"Have you got torches?" Rafiq asked him. "It's impossible to see anything in here. We don't even know where to begin looking."

Ahmed grinned sheepishly. "I knew there was something I had to bring."

Rafiq shook his head. "I'll get them. You keep looking."

He grabbed an empty sack lying on the ground and folded the coarse material into a head covering for himself. There were torches in the kitchen area, so he struggled across the compound towards the cooking hearths. It was easier this time because the wind was behind him and he was half blown along, the wind-carried sand now stinging his calves. Through the thick veil of lifted sand he could see beams of light swinging wildly from the direction of the communications hut as men worked at lashing down extra corrugated sheeting on the roof and walls. It was located at the centre of the compound, surrounded by the other huts to give it greater protection, and was made with the heaviest walls, the newest materials, the strongest door. It was always guarded.

Rafiq ducked in behind the screens that partitioned the cooking area and the family living quarters from the rest of the camp. He found two large torches stored behind the cooking pots and grabbed them both, tucking them under his sacking cape.

The first flash came as he was turning to leave the kitchen area. Everything was momentarily lit with a strange blue light. It caught Rafiq off guard and he halted. A second later the boom of the explosion reached his ears, loud even above the unceasing roar of the wind.

Immediately Rafiq dropped to his knees and lay prone, his eyes darting around, although from his concealed position behind the screens he couldn't see much. Keeping low, he edged forward, pulling himself along on his elbows, until his face was pressed against the woven screen. He could see sporadic muzzle flashes through the whipped-up sand and could hear the crack of gunfire, strangely dulled by the thickened air. There was shouting too, and shadowy figures running through the storm.

Rafiq's first thought was that there had been an accident with explosives in the munitions store. There was another flash. In the vivid blue light he saw the stores where he had been rummaging with Ahmed not five minutes before blast apart with the tremendous force of a massive explosion.

They were under attack.

The door of the store cabin shot upwards into the air and the corrugated roof whipped off, cartwheeling crazily into the darkness. Sacks of maize and rolls of plastic sheeting, crates of tools and bags of flour fountained skywards, ripped apart, incinerating into spinning balls of fire and plumes of black smoke. In the madness Rafiq saw Ahmed's body thumping down in the centre of the compound, twisted and mutilated. He felt a sickness in his belly.

There were more flashes and wild bursts of machine-gun fire as the attack intensified. The screen that sheltered him shuddered and splintered as bullets hit. Unknown men appeared, first in small groups of two or three, then more, spilling into the compound, firing indiscriminately at anything that moved. Rafiq could see their sand-coloured uniforms now, solid shapes emerging from the wildly swirling dust so that it seemed the invaders were materializing out of the storm itself.

Hut doors in the main compound opened into the blast of the storm and sleepy boys and men wandered out, curious about the noise, only to be gunned down by a torrent of machine-gun fire so they collapsed and fell dead in the doorways. Grenades lobbed into huts flashed blue, followed by loud explosions and shrieking. Fires blazed in bombed-out huts, lighting up the carnage and devastation.

The lights that had been swinging about at the communications hut had gone out. Any of Rafiq's brothers left alive were nowhere to be seen. They had melted into the million grains of stinging sand from which the new enemy was emerging.

Rafiq tried to make sense of what he was seeing. In the family quarters behind him he could hear panicked voices, movements, a child's cry. Light shone briefly through the cracks around the doors. The women were not permitted to appear in the main compound without their husbands but they would come out of their huts and hide behind the screens to see what the commotion was about. Their screams and the cries of little children would draw the gunmen to where he was hiding. They would be the next targets, and then it might be too late for Rafiq.

He had to get out of there.

Slithering like a snake in the sand-filled moonlight, he crawled deeper into the darkness, away from the huts as the cries and gunfire continued behind him. He headed for higher ground, grateful for the old brown sack that camouflaged him, and didn't look back until he reached the crest of the hill behind the camp. There he crawled behind some boulders, wrapped the sackcloth around him and stared numbly at the scene below.

The camp was brightly lit now by dozens of burning fires. The soldiers ran from hut to hut, lobbing in grenades and occasionally stopping to blast their guns at some fleeing boy or to torch one of the flimsy buildings. Rafiq could see the dead bodies of his brothers strewn around. Women and children lay dead on the ground in the cooking area, their clothing flapping wildly in the wind.

The army was crawling all over the camp. Soldiers surrounded the deserted communications hut. They did not burn it. Instead a small group ran in with sheets of plastic and emerged shortly afterwards, carrying the fragile apparatus into the night: the computer, the radio, the video camera, the satellite phone system.

Rafiq watched, his thoughts racing. He knew that the army must be based close by. This was no lucky strike. They had been watching, waiting for the right moment. They were taking no hostages or prisoners; this was a complete wipeout. Obliterate the camp. Burn any structures. Kill all militants. Those were their orders. What better night to attack than when there was a fierce dust storm? Their gods were with them, Rafiq thought sourly. Although it made their job tougher, the storm worked in their favour. Their advance had been completely drowned by the scream of the wind and the natural camouflage of dust.

Once the communications hut had been ransacked and the other huts torched, Rafiq saw the soldiers gathering around one man. The commander shouted orders and made sweeping movements with his arms. He sent the soldiers running in all directions from the camp, spreading in an ever-widening circle, to blanket search the surrounding area for any rogue fighters who had managed to escape the attack.

Rafiq knew his time for watching was over. He had to leave. He gathered his sackcloth about his shoulders, turned his back on the burning camp and threaded his way through the boulders and further into the darkness. Although it was pitch black on the far side of the hill, Rafiq would have been able to follow the route blindfolded. He began dropping down into the deep valley behind the mountain, crossing the camp's small river from where he knew there was a trail that led to caves less than half a day away. He would be there by morning.

18

It was the cool season in the fifth year since Rafiq's capture. Jameela was at home with her mother and Afrah. Her two brothers were in school, while their father was working in the shop. Jameela and Afrah had been washing clothes all morning in the courtyard, and now they were hanging the clean hijabs and skirts, shalwars and shirts over the washing rope strung from the walnut tree to the corner of the house. Their mother had winched the rope down for them to reach, and now that it was full of dripping clothes, she wound the stiff handle slowly to raise them up. The clothes snapped as the breeze caught them, spraying out droplets of water.

"They should dry quickly. It's a good wind," she said as Afrah emptied the soapy washing water onto the roots of the tree.

"I'll get the bedclothes." Jameela went into the house.

When she returned with her arms full of blankets and sleeping mats, her mother and Afrah were talking to a woman who had come into their courtyard. Jameela recognized her immediately as the mother of a stolen son. Since her child had been snatched, this woman was regularly seen around the village, bareheaded and unkempt, keening and wailing until late at night, or until her weary husband dragged her home because it was dark, there was no food prepared in her house and she was shaming him. Even now, her scarf was slipping from her hair, which was trailing untidily across her face. Jameela heaped the bedding onto the back step and joined them to hear any news.

"The army has raided a militants' camp high in the Pir Panjals," her mother said to her.

Jameela breathed in sharply. There had been no discussion of Rafiq and no news from the police for years. Now this. Suddenly. Unexpectedly.

The woman turned to Jameela, her eyes unnaturally bright, her body twitching and agitating as if her bones could find no peace.

"They found boys up there. Children as young as ten or eleven, with guns and grenades and bullets," she told Jameela, eager to have her story heard.

"Where did you hear this?"

"The police told me yesterday when I went to the station in Varahamula. The raid was almost a week ago."

The woman spoke quickly, tripping over her words with excitement. Jameela glanced at her mother before asking if any older boys had been found. Little children were of no interest to her. The woman sniggered, which startled Jameela.

"There were," she spluttered. "They mentioned boys of fourteen, fifteen."

"How did they find the camp?" Jameela's mother asked gently.

"Do you remember the attacks on the temple and the cloth bazaar in Poonch? It was months back."

They nodded, recalling the savage attack that had left dozens dead and wounded; men and women, children too. But Poonch was on the far side of the mountains, nowhere they had ever been.

"They caught one of the boys involved; he was captured running through the dark streets afterwards, trying to get back to his friends. He was all fire and fury when they first got him – waving his gun around and shouting. But they broke him quickly. He told them all about the camp and the militants."

"Is he still alive?" Afrah asked.

"As far as I know," the woman said, her arms fluttering and her head dipping as she replied. "He's not one of ours, though – I asked. He's young: no more than ten or eleven. With mountain features and no knowledge of the low plains."

"How far away is this camp?" asked Jameela. Perhaps she could go there on the bus. She was older now, well able to travel. Her mother might come too.

"Far, far away," the woman told her. "High up in the windswept mountains where the peaks are covered in snow all year round."

Jameela had only seen those mountains in the purple-hazed distance, with their forbidding white summits nudging aggressively into the sky, piercing the soft clouds. She couldn't imagine her brother living up there. She couldn't imagine any person living up there.

"The police told the army. They found the camp. It was big, spread over a wide area, full of boys and men. They found weapons there. Equipment too."

"Were any of the older boys captured alive?" Jameela's mother asked softly.

The woman cackled again, a wild, strange sound that didn't fit with the conversation.

"Don't know yet. Maybe. We'll have to see. We might be lucky." She stepped back a little, itching to leave. "I've more people to tell. Can't stay. Can't delay."

And with that she hurried off, her movements uncomfortable to watch. When she had gone, Afrah spoke.

"That woman is so strange." She imitated her jerkiness, giggling. "All wriggles and jumps."

Her mother started untangling the heap of blankets and mattresses, which she spread along the top of the wall to air in the sun.

"She's had it hard. She has no other children, just the one son. He was her life. He was fourteen at the time of the stealing and his marriage had already been arranged.

It was a good match. I remember her telling me the news. She was full of pride, with the wedding planned to take place within two years. But now it'll never happen. She has nothing left in her life."

Jameela leaned across and took some of the blankets from her mother.

"Do you think Rafiq was in that camp, Mamma? One of the boys they found there?"

"I don't know, Jameela."

She stopped her work, took down her scarf and ran a hand through her hair. For the first time, Jameela noticed a strand of silver streaking her glossy black hair. Her mother looked old, sad. Worn out. The whole business with Rafiq had wearied her.

"She did mention fourteen-year-olds. Just think. My Rafiq. Fourteen years old now. Almost a man."

"Maybe we should go ourselves to the police station and find out what happened up in that camp?" suggested Jameela. "Perhaps they have captives. Perhaps they have names, details."

She was burning to find out more. It was the first spark of hope in the five empty years since he'd gone missing. She had to find out if anyone had come out alive from that high cold place where her brother might have been living.

"I don't know, Jameela." Her mother hesitated. "What about your father? He's decided that Rafiq is no longer part of our family. I can't even tell him what we heard today. What would he say?"

Jameela stood in front of her mother, almost the same height as her now, and smiled. She took her mother's hands – strong hands, but rough, the knuckles swollen and knobbly.

"But Rafiq will always be part of our family," she whispered. "*You* know that."

Her mother nodded, her eyes soft as butter. Jameela continued, her tone gentle and coaxing.

"And when we find out something strong and good about him, it will melt Papa's heart and he'll want his true first son home again. But until then, we don't need to tell him everything we're up to."

Her mother's eyes opened wide. She snatched back her hands and covered her mouth.

"Jameela! He's my husband. I can't deceive him."

"What?" Afrah piped up, dancing over to where they stood. "You trick him all the time! I remember you bought a pencil and notebook for Jameela and told Papa the onions and tomatoes cost extra. And what about when I scorched his prayer mat with the lantern? You told him the goat ate it."

Jameela joined in, smiling now. "Remember you gave eggs to that poor woman who came begging a few weeks ago? When Papa wanted fresh eggs, you told him that the kid goat had stepped on them and smashed them."

Their mother laughed at her two daughters. "I blame the poor goats for a lot," she said. "It's just as well they can't speak for themselves. But this is different. Hiding a few small things is how we get by, but asking about my son in the big police station in Varahamula…" She shook her head as she thought of it. "What would he say if he found out?"

"He won't find out, Mamma. I'll cover for you and Jameela," said Afrah. "Go to the market as normal, then visit the police station. You can still be on the same bus home and Papa won't know any different. I'll stay here and cook the evening meal and take care of the boys."

Jameela looked at her little sister. She was only eight. She was trying to be strong, but it was too much to expect her to prepare and cook food for her father and two brothers.

"I'll make the food the night before, Afrah, so that you only need to heat it up. We can leave the pots in the cold store until the next evening."

Afrah smiled gratefully at Jameela, while their mother held her hands up to her face. She was worried, but it seemed as though her two capable daughters had decided everything. Jameela looked at her and smiled.

"All you have to do is come with me on the bus," she said.

And so it was settled.

19

Since his escape Rafiq hadn't emerged during daylight. He spent the long hot hours resting in the shady interior of the cave. Sleep wasn't possible because his limbs twitched at the slightest sound. His eyes flickered restlessly over the empty hills, always alert for soldiers creeping up on him. He watched the scorpions skulk beneath the boulders and the black bats that hung from the rocky roof. The cave stank from the bat droppings that littered the ground and Rafiq had had to find an overhang within the cave so they didn't fall on him where he lay. Sometimes he dozed on the sandy floor, startling awake whenever the slightest breeze grazed his damp skin. He had not eaten at all since he fled the camp but his belly wasn't looking for food. Instead his heart looked constantly for answers.

He had no weapons. He struggled to recall a time

when he was last without his gun or, at the very least, a sharp dagger in his belt. He felt exposed and vulnerable, his belt strangely light without its bullets or grenades, his hands restless.

During the first freezing night in the cave, he sat trembling, staring into the star-pierced darkness, his body stiff and inert. All through the black night, flashing images and silent screams filled his head. They grew more vivid and terrifying whenever he closed his eyes, and so he didn't. He stayed upright against the boulders, afraid to sleep, afraid even to blink, so that when the sun ripened the air and warmed the ground, his eyes were burning and raw.

The next night, he crept out and searched close to the cave for kindling. Heaping it together, he scooped dried bat droppings into the pile and used the batteries from the torches he had brought to throw sparks and light the twigs. The fire took hold and the jumping flames stopped his limbs from shivering. Spirits were clamouring in his head, but the firelight soothed them and their howling voices softened. Rafiq slumped against a boulder and stared listlessly at the small blaze.

But something seemed to happen in the fire, deep within its shimmering heart.

The longer he looked, the more certain he became that silhouettes of the other freedom fighters were leaping among the ribbons of flame. Their shadows cavorted around the walls of the cave, distorted into grotesque shapes by the rocks.

Rafiq was at first mesmerized by the sight and stared, trying to interpret what it meant. But as he watched, he became certain that their writhing movements were tortured, agonized dances of death. He was convinced that he saw his comrades fleeing the firestorm of the camp. When he realized this, a cold fear gripped him and he went rigid with shock.

He leaped to his feet and kicked savagely at the fire, scattering flaming missiles throughout the cave. He stamped frantically at each miniature blaze, grinding it into the dust until it was no more than a charred smudge. When the fire was completely quenched and the cave was in darkness once again, Rafiq dropped to his knees and prayed for forgiveness from his brothers for making them relive the torment of the attack.

He lit no more fires. Instead he tried to focus his mind by praying and disciplining his thoughts, but found it impossible to push back the strange feelings that confused him. Being entirely alone was something new to him. He had never before slept alone, never before existed for a day on his own, never before communicated with only himself. And he found the long isolated days harrowing. Every slow minute bored into his solitary soul and dragged haunting thoughts to the surface. In sleep, and even when awake, images danced before his eyes: vague disturbing recollections of dreams from a different time, a different place; fractured memories of a childhood that might have been. Plum trees blossomed in a shaded square, only to be replaced by wild mountains and white-iced peaks. Faces emerged: some he recognized, others nudging uncomfortably on the periphery of his memory, lost and broken.

He wondered if he was the only one of the fighters to survive. The caves were a known refuge and he had expected others to join him, but no one did. There were other hideouts in the mountains: abandoned shepherd huts, ancient stone dwellings from prehistoric tribes, and bigger honeycomb caves further away. His brothers might be hiding out in any of them, but he doubted it.

Ahmed was dead. A holy martyr, a life given for God's war. It was a great end, but Rafiq felt no joy. Neither did he feel sadness. He felt empty inside, hollow, as though there were nothing there. His thoughts grew dull and unfocused, as if the inertia from his limbs had crept into his skull and deadened his mind.

On the third morning, he walked out of his hideout into the bright sunshine and began the half-day trek to the camp. The sun was white and hard, forcing him to squint, and the ground was rough, but Rafiq barely felt the sharp gravel and splinters of stone. Gradually the sun stole the chill from the early morning, and before long he was sweating. His head started to ache. He needed to drink.

Eventually he reached the source of the river that fed the camp. He stopped and squinted at the surrounding hills, searching for moving figures, for any signs of life. He saw only wild mountain goats in the distance. Satisfied, he squatted down and cupped his grimy hands into the pool, drinking deeply. He washed off some of the filth of the last few days, scrubbing his skin with sand and dunking his head to rinse the grit and dust from his hair. Then he continued on his way, checking repeatedly for movement in the hills.

The light had shifted from white to soft gold when the hills took on familiar shapes, clean contours that he recognized. The breeze carried on it a lingering smell of burning and, beneath it, the sickening breath of decay.

At the final hill overlooking the huts Rafiq dropped to the ground and cautiously bellied his way to the top. Hardly a pebble rolled or clicked against its companions as he slithered over the crest. He could see the charred huts now, some of them still smouldering even after three days. The roofs of those left standing were blackened. Smoke curled from heaps of rubble. The detritus of people's lives lay scattered on the ground, wrecked and useless: cooking pots, sleeping mats. He could see bodies, abandoned where they had fallen, clothing still fluttering in the light breeze.

All was silent, but the atmosphere was thick and malodorous with the violence that had visited the place.

Rafiq felt a sharp pain inside himself when he looked at the destruction of his home. His blood thickened and his muscles felt weak. He was unable to move any closer and didn't know what to do. There was no one to tell him. All he could do was crouch behind the boulders and stare bleakly at the violated site. He saw no one. Nothing disturbed the appalling scene.

The sunlight deepened and still he sat, numbed, in the shelter of the scattered rocks. When shadows began to break the light apart, he slowly pulled himself up. Keeping alert and vigilant, he edged towards the camp. The stench grew stronger and he paused to pull a fluttering piece of cloth, snagged on a twisted branch, to wrap across his face.

He walked around desolately, tracing the worn paths from kitchen area to stores, from sleeping huts to central compound, from communications hut to family quarters. All of the cabins had been ransacked; most had been completely emptied, if not by the army, then by local hill tribes. The animal pens were bare, and even the assault course had been dismantled: ropes slashed, poles smashed, netting cut to shreds. In every place were the charred corpses of men, women and children.

For the first time in his life, Rafiq found the carnage harrowing. Death was something he was used to, but this was personal. He passed the blackened fire area. He skirted the bodies of his brothers: some he had trained, some who had trained him, some too young to have even started training. The air was thick with fat flies that buzzed lazily.

He stepped over Ahmed's twisted and swollen corpse lying face downwards in the dirt and paused to look on him. Rafiq's breathing became laboured; he struggled to fill his lungs. He felt an ache spreading through his limbs, a tightness rising in his throat, and hurtling thoughts crowded his head. Ahmed had been the nearest thing to a friend he'd had. This camp had been their home for five years. Although Rafiq didn't associate it with happiness, it had been his life and these were his brothers, his family, who had been taken from him.

He scanned the ruined settlement, the dead bodies, the empty mountains. And he sobbed: a harsh cry that shook his shoulders and shuddered his entire body. Anguish and loss were not new to him, but this time they reached into his broken soul, exhausting it of whatever spirit remained. He fell to his knees in the stony dirt and dropped his head, unable to see beyond the moment he was in. What was left to him? He had no people. He had no future.

Rafiq considered his brothers and their glorious end. They had died for Kashmir, for Allah, as had been their destiny. They were together now, magnificent martyrs in paradise. And what had he achieved? There was nothing left for him in this life.

But he could still achieve something. He could avenge their deaths. He could fight for his dead brothers. He took a deep breath and resolved to be strong. He was a soldier, fighting for the freedom of Kashmir. For his own true freedom. With these thoughts his broken heart hardened. They fuelled a wrath gathering inside him until it sang in his bones and heated his blood.

Moving away from Ahmed's body, he continued along the path with purpose now as his thoughts quickened. He searched for signs that anyone had survived, but he found nothing but rotting corpses and creeping rats which had already invaded the abandoned space and were scratching in the shadows, perturbed by his presence. He shifted his focus to a search for useful articles to take.

Entering the cooking area, he rummaged among the broken pottery and eventually found a few rounds of stale bread and a cracked bowl of cooked cornmeal. Scattering the rats, he ate handfuls of it, stuffing it into his mouth. He broke the hard bread into chunks, which he sucked, and tore apart two oranges, dried and shrivelled from the sun.

Hoping there might be more provisions in the women's quarters, Rafiq entered their cabins with a brief supplication, and retrieved two scorched blankets, a damaged kerosene stove, wicks and matches. He found loose onions and a small sack of potatoes and moved to and from the central compound, heaping everything together. He would decide later what to take with him.

He was emerging for the third time, his arms full of sleeping mats, when he was startled by something moving around the perimeter of the settlement.

There was a scuttling shadow, then the dry scraping of rocks and the sound of breathing.

Rafiq dropped what he was carrying and crouched low to the ground, furious with himself for failing to find a weapon when he first arrived. Ducking into the hut, he frantically cast his eyes around and found some shards of broken pottery, sharp enough to use if he had to defend himself. He stood still and listened, holding his breath.

Feet scuffed against rocks. Something smashed as it was knocked over. The movements were noisy and careless. Closer this time. No effort was made to tread softly.

The hairs on the back of Rafiq's neck prickled as he saw a shadow slide slowly through the gap between his hut and the adjacent one. Seconds later, there was a loud snort as one of the camp horses wandered nonchalantly into the central compound. Rafiq's taut muscles relaxed and he smiled with relief when he realized his foolishness. Dropping his pottery weapons, he ran to the startled animal and grabbed the rope tied around its neck, laughing into the strong sweaty flank.

He tethered the horse, then went in search of something with which to protect himself but the army had stripped the place of guns and weapons. He ran to the stores where Ahmed and he had been rummaging on the night of the attack, but nothing useful remained. There was nothing where the store cabin had once stood, except for a bizarre blackened square burnt onto the whispering sand.

Rafiq thought of Ahmed. Perhaps he'd carried a gun or a knife. He returned to the body, kneeled down and searched it, his hands flitting lightly across the clothing. Tucked into the belt, wrapped in an orange bandanna, was a small knife. Rafiq held it up and its honed blade flashed in the sun. Allah was smiling on him this time. He stashed it in his own belt and tied the bandanna around his face, flinging aside the torn cloth. Now he felt stronger. With a knife, a bandanna and a horse, anything was possible, and a plan was already forming in Rafiq's bitter thoughts.

Before he left the body, he looked down at Ahmed's feet and, after a moment's hesitation, prised the plastic sandals off and slipped them on himself.

Rafiq wanted to be away from this place of death before dark in case the spirits of the dead came to reclaim their bodies. Tying the food and other essentials into one of the blankets, he threw the pack over the haunches of the horse, then tossed the other blanket onto the animal's bare back and leaped on.

Rafiq steered his mount towards a cluster of rocks a short distance away. Once there, he stopped and stared. Abdullah's lifeless body lay crumpled in a heap in the dirt. Bloodstains darkened the earth. A chill breeze ruffled the air and rippled the clothing on the corpse. Hauling the body aside, Rafiq was relieved to see that the earth beneath it had not been unduly disturbed. He scrabbled around until he found what he was looking for: a rusted iron ring embedded in the ground. He hauled on it, throwing his entire weight against the hoop until a wooden trapdoor creaked upwards, cascading grit and sand into the hole. It crashed back onto the dirt, clouds of dust filling the air. Rafiq peered into the black hole revealed beneath. In spite of its thorough sweeps of the area, the army had not found the munitions store.

Rafiq kneeled down and scooped out grenades, plastic explosives, detonators, rifles, rounds of bullets. He took two heavy knives and a sharpening stone. He found empty canvas sacks, which he filled with the weapons and ammunition, and loaded up the horse.

As night crept through the mountains, cooling the air with the spirits of the dead, Rafiq cantered his horse through the shadows, which crept into his soul until he felt as if he were dissolving into the darkness.

20

At the start of his trek Rafiq travelled under cover of darkness so he wouldn't be seen. Local people would know his distinctive bandanna, maybe even recognize the horse, and he didn't want to be identified as coming from the camp. Once the night sky was fully spread, he rode for several hours until exhaustion overtook him.

He settled the horse under a copse of trees. He gathered twigs and sticks and built a small pyramid with them, stuffing dry grasses into the centre. But he couldn't bring himself to light the fire. Instead he stood and stared at the heap of kindling, hovering around it anxiously, wondering if his brothers' restless spirits were in there, ready to leap out of the flames again, ready to relive the agony of their deaths. He looked up at the starry heavens, where a cold moon shone, staining the sky white, and walked around the sticks. The temperature dropped. He moved his belongings closer and pulled up the collar of his thin shirt. His stomach growled with hunger.

Sitting down and unrolling his pack, he removed some onions and potatoes, lined them up and looked at them hungrily. He even sliced a chunk of raw potato and sucked it, but the starch was bitter and chalked his mouth. He spat it out and stood up again. And finally made the decision.

Unwilling to let fear command his thoughts, he snatched up a match, struck it and lit the dry grasses in one quick movement. They shrank and sizzled, black fragments tumbling off the ends, before they caught and glowed brightly. The burn rushed to the heart of the kindling. Rafiq squatted low and watched apprehensively as tiny flames sprang out, snapping around the twigs, feeding on them. The blaze leaped upwards, its warmth comforting, but he couldn't relax. He fretted and worried; he unfurled his clenched fingers. He stared nervously at the flames, searching for ghosts, but all he could see was an ordinary blaze.

Gradually he dropped his hunched shoulders and moved off his hunkers to sit on the blanket. As the bigger sticks caught and the fire settled, he put his onions and potatoes onto flat stones and pushed them into the shimmering heat. He took them out when they were blistered black with steaming centres that scorched his tongue because he was too hungry to wait for them to cool.

His eyes felt heavy and he stretched out. At last sleep

came, swiftly sending him into an oblivion that brought temporary relief.

When his food supply ran out, Rafiq pilfered from outhouses and sheds while people slept. He had learned from the militants not to strip one place bare. These were poor people. So he crept through several homes each night, taking a few eggs here, some carrots there. He didn't need much.

As he moved further from the high settlement, the snowy peaks receded and the vegetation increased. The nights grew warmer, with a damp heat heralding the start of day. He passed into the foothills, then travelled through flat open plains and farmed lands. He took to riding during the early morning when the misty light seeped into the darkness, and again in the evening when the heat of the sun cooled.

The long days on his own seemed all the longer with only his bleak thoughts for company. Everything took so much time to work out, because he had to fight through a fog of sadness and lost memories. It was a struggle for him and he put a great deal of effort into each small decision, like where to stop for the night. Often he settled in one spot, rolling out his blanket and gathering kindling for a fire, only to decide that another place would give him more shelter, or provide him with a better view of the road. He'd have to move then, taking up his belongings, untying his horse and riding onwards.

One night, he passed close to a small village, no more than a cluster of houses set around an old stone well.

A bright moon split everything into silver light and black shadow. He tethered his horse and went to the well first, padding softly over the smooth flagstones. A goat bleated from behind one of the houses, immediately putting him in mind of sweet milk, warm and fresh. He turned his head to locate it, and his sharp eye spotted a house with an open window. He stepped closer. There was probably food in there: perhaps fresh curd, spiced fruit or chicken stew.

Rafiq paused, wondering which house he should choose. The goat bleated again, telling him its whereabouts. But the open window was wide, drawing him closer. Still he stood, his forehead creased, perplexed by the choice facing him, a choice so difficult that he could do nothing but stand helplessly as confusion and uncertainty bubbled inside him.

He forced himself to move and stepped tentatively towards the open window. He gazed in at a small cooking area curtained off from the rest of the house. He hadn't seen inside a home like this for many years. A strange sensation wormed uneasily through his stomach as he was distracted by the warm glow from the small fire in the clay stove. It looked comforting. He could see earthenware vessels stacked in the corner, and the sweet smells of cinnamon and cardamom wafted out. He stood motionless for a long time, staring blankly, his thoughts crowded with some other long-forgotten cooking pots, some other clay oven, his hands hanging slack at his sides.

His horse snorted unexpectedly and Rafiq blinked.

The spell was broken. He looked and saw that the moon was already sinking. His feet were numb from standing still for so long. He walked softly, slowly, from that village, bringing neither goat's milk nor newly turned curd but a head filled with images of a warm home and the trappings of family life.

Delaying, lingering, indecision. These had never been problems when Rafiq had lived at the camp. He didn't recall ever before struggling with irrelevant details. He just got on with things; did as he was told; smartly followed orders. It was simple, uncomplicated. There were no confusing choices, no intruding memories. This new daily struggle with unimportant things irritated and frustrated him. He sat on his horse, riding at dawn or dusk, and stared bleakly ahead, trying to work out why his life had become so difficult. Why did he have to struggle to get up in the morning, his eyelids heavy and his limbs sluggish? Why did he stare for half the dawn into the cold grey ash of last night's fire, instead of jumping on his horse and continuing his journey?

The only thoughts that fired him and made him feel alive were those about planning his mission. That occupied many, many hours. He was still a true Kashmiri soldier: that could never be taken away from him; and that was why it was easy for him to work out his plan. Physical limitations like tiredness meant nothing when he was fighting the war to free his country, to avenge his murdered brothers.

From the moment the hot spark of anger had ignited his forlorn spirit as he explored the ruined settlement, he knew his reprisal had to be simple, direct and easily executed by a single soldier. He was a solo combatant now. This time, there would be no decoys or secondary attacks. There would be one opportunity; one revenge hit; one final strike that would bring Rafiq the ultimate glory. The struggle of decision-making fell away and his mind leapt into action as he considered what the target should be and how best to use his cache of weapons.

Once he was out of the high mountains, Rafiq's route was easy and his horse trotted along with no trouble, following the banks of the meandering river that led to Varahamula. He arrived in the depths of night. The streets were dark and quiet.

Rafiq remembered when he had been in Poonch with Kareem and Samir to attack the temple. He recalled the narrow streets, the confusing alleyways, the endless wait for a boy soldier who had not returned. The streets here looked the same, with their yapping dogs and puddles of foul water. Rafiq dismounted and led his horse by its reins, heading for the centre. He had decided his target.

He passed sleeping households and slumbering street dwellers. The horse's hooves echoed eerily along the surfaced road leading towards the main chowk. At several corners he saw people sleeping in small knots of four and five, probably families, their heads and bodies completely shrouded in blankets. Occasionally a blanket corner lifted and a silent face peered out, watching him go by.

Before reaching the chowk, Rafiq passed a stretch of

battered hoarding. He ambled past slowly, his eyes flitting around, searching the adjacent doorways and corners for sleeping people, but seeing none. He sniffed the air for smells of fires or food, but detected nothing. Slowly, at the next junction, he turned and led his horse back. He scrutinized the hoarding carefully, circling its perimeter. There were one or two places where it bowed and cracked, gaping wide enough to admit a boy and perhaps even a horse. Leaving his horse cropping weeds, he squeezed through and peered around. There were no street dwellers in here; it would suit his needs perfectly.

Rafiq emerged and again checked the streets all around, then hefted his weight against a length of the hoarding. It curved and groaned until something gave way and the entire board buckled, then creaked noisily to one side. Small stones beneath it exploded as they were crushed. His horse whinnied in alarm.

Rafiq froze. He held his breath, but nobody appeared to see what the racket was about. Cautiously he clambered through, his feet crunching on twisted wire and crushed stone, this time dragging his reluctant horse behind him.

Rafiq quickly untied the sacks bulging with explosives. He squatted down and dug a hiding place among heaps of broken tiling and crumbled bricks, sliding in the ammunition and stacking more shattered ceramics on top until it was buried completely.

Stepping lightly across the teetering rubble, he led his horse back to the wrecked hoarding. His heart hammered in his chest and his eyes strained against the limits of the darkness, but the road was empty, the street lights gleaming coldly onto bare concrete. He scrambled out with his horse and dragged the hoarding back into place, so it appeared not to have been disturbed. Then he continued along the road, arriving shortly at the chowk, where the White Mosque dominated the vista, glowing softly in the dark. Rafiq paused to look at the beautiful building, sensing the sacred space surrounding it calm his beating heart. Tomorrow, before his strike, he would visit and pray for success in his mission.

In the chowk masses of stalls were in place for the next day. It was fortunate, Rafiq thought, to arrive on the eve of market day. The town would be thronging not only with locals, but with villagers and visiting merchants carrying out their business. Rafiq stared at the rows of wooden shacks, their counters bolted shut for the night, their canopies fluttering like black veils. The fragrance of the fresh foods laid out for sale carried on the light breeze.

At one fruit stall Rafiq inhaled the clean perfume of oranges and bright mint leaves, cardamom and glowing apricots. His stomach was empty. He had not eaten that day and cast around in the hope of finding something to pilfer; but beneath almost every lean-to he could see the legs and feet of the sleeping owner poking out. He couldn't risk being chased, so he ignored his growling belly and continued circling the chowk until he came to the town's main police station.

Leaving his horse tethered to a post, he investigated the perimeter of the ugly building, examining its doors and windows. He stood in front of it and eyed its vast width and imposing height. He counted the steps to the main entrance; he paced the streets to its left, to its right. Finally he climbed its worn steps and rattled the securely locked door to check its strength, before turning to look down at the cluttered chowk. All these things would determine the scale of his attack.

Retrieving his horse, he wandered around for a while, not sure where to go, a lost boy padding through the silent streets. In a narrow back alley with small windows high up in the surrounding walls, he tied his horse to a ring set into the brick and cast his eye around, but there was no obvious corner in which he could curl up and doze. Without thinking, he found himself drawn back to the fruit stall, seeking something that reminded him of the clean air of his mountain home.

Behind the stall was an ancient stone portico, its porch deep and sheltered. Rafiq lowered himself wearily onto the worn steps, and found shelter in the shadow of the imposing brass door, from where he could smell the fresh fruit. He would lie quietly until the day was hot and teeming and fully awake.

As he leaned his head back, Rafiq looked up at the sky, where the stars were beginning to lose their sparkle.

Soon he would make his revenge strike.

21

Afrah got up even earlier than Jameela and her mother, too excited and nervous to sleep any longer. She was lighting the kerosene lamp when Jameela filled the little metal basin with water and went outside to the courtyard to wash. She looked up at the stars and saw that they were beginning to lose their sparkle as the night gave birth to a new day. By the time she returned, Afrah was preparing chapattis and hot tea for breakfast. They all three squatted in silence on the rug, chewing warm chapattis, each lost in her own thoughts. Their mother was the first to blink and stretch.

"We'd better go," she said, adjusting her scarf around her head and taking up her basket.

Jameela nodded, put down her tea and stood up. It was still dark outside, although the sky in the east was streaked with yellow and grey.

"Bring home my brother," Afrah whispered to them at the door. "I hardly remember him and want to see what he looks like."

Jameela hushed her, afraid their father would hear.

"Don't forget to collect the eggs for Papa," she told Afrah, changing the subject. "And Mahmood likes lots of sugar in his lemon tea."

Afrah laughed and pushed her away. "Stop fussing. I can take care of things here. Now, go!"

Her mother spoke seriously to her young daughter. "If we are late home for any reason, I have left extra food in the cold store. If you don't open the door to let flies in, it should be fine until tonight, although you will have to prepare rice. There is curd already turning in the butter bowl. It should be good by the time you are ready to eat."

Afrah nodded, smoothing out creases in her mother's skirt. Secretly she was excited about running the house for the day. "It'll be fine. Papa won't suspect a thing."

As Jameela and her mother hurried down the street to the junction where the bus stopped, they met other women scuttling through the darkness to the same spot, some carrying packages and parcels of food to sell. The bus was packed by the time it reached their village. Jameela and her mother crammed on, along with the other village women, and paid their fares. Jameela sat on top of a sack of flour stored in the aisle, while her mother squeezed in with two women and a baby in a seat intended for two.

They had their day carefully planned. Varahamula

was always crowded on market day. People from outlying villages attended to all their business and there would be long queues everywhere, including the police station. They decided to go there first to try to get ahead of the crowd. Afterwards they would do a few small errands to make the journey appear authentic.

"We'll buy some fruit," Jameela's mother decided. "Your papa loves apples and it'll please him if I bring them home."

"And oranges and peaches," Jameela added.

They could make all their purchases at one stall, saving precious time.

They were not the only ones from their village that morning with the same mission in mind. Several women had decided to travel to the town following the woman's story about the raid on the mountain settlement. The bus was full of anticipation and excited chatter.

"I heard there are boy prisoners being held in the police station," one woman announced to no one in particular.

"No? I never heard that. I thought no one was caught."

"There had better be boys in the police station," another woman interrupted loudly. "Otherwise this will be a wasted journey for all of us."

"No journey about my boys is wasted. I could rest easy if I just knew they were alive."

"My husband thinks I've gone to buy rice and kerosene."

"Mine thinks I'm selling wool at the market. He didn't seem to notice that I've none to sell."

Most of the men in the village appeared to know nothing about the plans of their women.

Jameela listened to the rise and fall of chatter, staring out of the window as the bus lumbered along the road leading to the mountains. With the brightening of the day, she felt her sleepiness disappear like the lost dawn. She was nervous and excited, her stomach fluttering and her thoughts racing with images of her brother. She imagined meeting him and wondered what she'd say to him. What he'd say to her. Would he look so different?

"Don't be silly, Jameela," Afrah had laughed as they'd talked about it together the previous day while milking the goats. "Of course he'll look different. It's five years later. He'll be all grown up and big."

Jameela had sighed, pressing her head against the soft flank of the nanny goat, which had bleated in response. "But how different? Will he still look like Rafiq, like one of our family ... or will he have a stranger's look in his eye?"

Afrah, who sometimes had the devil peeking through her own bright eyes, had lifted her head and rocked back on her wooden stool to look across at Jameela.

"Would you really know anyway? What if some strange boy *said* he was Rafiq? What if he wanted to live with us? Would you believe him? Would you bring him home?"

"No!" Jameela had abruptly stopped milking to stare at her grinning sister. "We couldn't let that happen. Some strange boy, some mountain soldier, in our home pretending to be Rafiq?"

Afrah's smile had faded then, and a kindness crept into her little face upon seeing her sister's reaction. "But it might happen. That strange boy might be our brother. Would you really know the true Rafiq?"

As the bus clattered its wheezy way through the mountains, twisting and turning, climbing and clunking, Jameela pondered Afrah's words. She closed her eyes and tried to remember his face. What made him unique? What made him her brother and not some stranger? But her memory of his features wasn't clear and sharp. It was soft around the edges and blurry in the middle, and Jameela felt the jitters rising from her toes as she imagined herself looking into the empty eyes of some unknown boy and being told it was Rafiq, being told he was returning to live with her family. How would she explain him to her brother and sister? To her unforgiving father?

"When we arrive," her mother whispered, leaning over and relieving Jameela of her anxious daydreams, "we'll catch a cycle rickshaw to the police station. It'll be much faster than walking. I have the money for it."

Jameela nodded, smiling at her mother even though fretfulness rippled through her like electricity. She wished they were there and the deed was done. It seemed the longest bus journey ever. In every village, they stopped for an age, the engine idling as people clambered on and off, or stood on the steps arguing with the driver about the fare, or climbed up on the roof to strap on parcels or sacks of vegetables.

At last, when the sun was smiling and the day was hot, the bus pulled into Varahamula station. Her mother was the first off, scuttling through the crowds, skilfully dodging buses and vehicles, while Jameela trotted after her. The rickshaws were bunched together at the far side of the bus station, their owners sitting on their cycles, touting for business. In one hot breath Jameela and her mother were surrounded by more than a dozen of them, pushing and shoving, grasping at their arms. Jameela pulled back, sheltering behind her mother.

"Yes, madam? You want rickshaw? This way. Very good, very good."

"My rickshaw is here, lady. Come now with your lovely daughter."

"Where to, madam? Your ears will be very happy with my price."

Jameela's mother negotiated a cheap fare with one of the men and they clambered into the back and set off, weaving through the dense traffic and blaring horns. The plastic seat was hot beneath them and Jameela gripped the side of the rickshaw as they rocked and swayed.

The streets were packed with people and lined with little huckster shops selling fruit, spices and hot pastries. The owner of each shop hunkered among his produce eyeing up the customers, shooing away children or dogs, shouting and bargaining hard to get the best prices. Locals tried to do their daily shopping, elbowing their way past people from out of town who had travelled since dawn to sell their goods and buy their monthly provisions before returning to distant mountains or villages. Jameela breathed in the smells of spices and foodstuffs, the hustle and bustle, as they whizzed past.

They reached the end of the street that opened into the main chowk, one side of which was dominated by the gleaming White Mosque that dazzled in the sun. Jameela had seen it before, but every time, it took her breath away.

"Isn't it beautiful?" she breathed, gazing up at the minaret that flashed brighter than the sun.

"Before we go home today," her mother replied, "we will visit here and pray together."

"Here is the police station, lady," the rickshaw cyclist announced as he drew up at a large squat building opposite the mosque. Before they had even paid and scrambled from the seat, the cyclist was shouting at another potential customer. He sped off into the thick traffic again without a backward glance.

"Do you think the people in this place know where Rafiq might be?" her mother asked as they both looked up at the concrete ugliness.

Jameela was afraid to answer. Afraid to speak her dreams aloud.

They climbed the steps together and tentatively pushed open the swing doors leading into the tiled lobby.

There were crowds of people already gathered there, queuing up to see two harassed officers in sweat-stained shirts, who were working in a large office behind the customer counter. The whole area was sweltering and malodorous. Although there were several fans turning lazily on the ceiling, they barely stirred the currents of hot air. They weren't even strong enough to dislodge the tattered cobwebs that clung to their yellowed sails.

Jameela and her mother joined those squatting or sitting around the stained walls. They settled their few belongings beside them and adjusted their veils. They would be waiting a long time, but they had the whole day. Although the police officers were busy typing on numerous sheets of fluttering paper, taking notes in huge dusty ledgers, making endless phone calls and hurrying in and out of the room, there appeared to be little or no progress in the disorderly queue. Phones rang constantly, harried voices called from distant rooms, footsteps hurried down unseen corridors, but hardly anyone was called to the counter. The people who were standing at it when Jameela first came in were still standing there an hour later.

"Are they all here to ask about the lost boys?" Jameela whispered to her mother, looking at the weary faces of the people ahead of them.

"I don't think so," her mother replied. "They are not from our village. They have other business for the police to deal with."

Jameela had never been to a police station before and wondered why so many people might need the services of the police. The lobby gradually became even more crowded as new arrivals trickled in. Jameela recognized some of them from the bus. At last one of the police officers called for the next in the line to come up, and everyone shifted slightly around the walls, rearranging themselves. Jameela knew they were next in the queue after a large family group who had entered the station just before them. It seemed like it was going to take for ever to be seen.

The drowsy morning wore on, the heat of the lobby adding to the lethargy of everyone in the queue. Jameela was sleepy. The alertness and anticipation she had felt on the bus were replaced by apathy as the day crawled on and in spite of herself she dozed off, her head lolling against her mother's shoulder. She awoke with a start when her mother dug her in the ribs because they needed to move round the walls again.

Jameela shuffled over and blinked, her dream of Rafiq still bright and alive in her memory. His face was now suddenly clear in her mind; she could see his quick smile and thick dark hair flopping across his forehead. This was a good sign, Jameela thought to herself. She stretched and smiled, the worry of Afrah's words fading, feeling reassured that she would recognize her brother when she saw him. She looked around the crowded lobby, at the faces of those other women and daughters who had travelled from their village to Varahamula, and wondered if they felt as hopeful as she did.

"Why don't you go and buy the fruit?" her mother suggested, holding out loose change. "In case we're delayed longer than expected. Nothing will move here for a while. You'll be back by the time we're called."

Jameela nodded, eager to escape the stale air of the station.

It was fresh outside after the stuffiness of the lobby and Jameela breathed deeply. She scanned the market for a fruit stall. Spotting one near the fringes, she skipped lightly down the steps and into the crowded chowk, pushing and squeezing her way through the surging crowds. She eventually reached her target stall, popping out from the masses to stand at its fruit-heavy counter.

The smell of the fresh produce lingered temptingly in the air and Jameela looked carefully over the display: baskets of oranges; dishes of apples, peaches and pears; bowls of figs and strawberries, cherries and dates. Picking up an empty basket, she selected a range of fruit, feeling for ripeness and checking for blemishes. If these were for her father, then only the best and sweetest could be chosen. Counting the money in her hand, she added two plump apricots for herself and her mother to enjoy while they waited in the police station.

The stall keeper was busy serving other customers, weighing out their goods, and as she waited, Jameela's gaze wandered idly. Behind the stall was a large portico leading into an old stone building. The imposing door looked ancient, with a great brass ring at its centre and a gleaming patina on its lower half from countless grasping hands clutching it over its lifetime. Jameela imagined the thousands of stories which that old door could recount, had it a voice of its own: of merchants and rich people who had entered beneath its decorative arch. She stood on her tiptoes to see the steps, knowing they too would be polished smooth, perhaps even dipping in the centre where the surface was worn from years of treading feet.

But her imaginings came to an abrupt halt when she saw that the steps were occupied. A scrawny beggar boy was curled on them, sleeping. Jameela stared at him, a sudden dampness creeping over her heart. She noticed his filthy feet and unkempt hair. A small dog was sniffing the ground next to him and Jameela felt a little comforted to know that the boy at least had the company of the animal.

"Are you next?"

The stall keeper's voice cut in on her thoughts, startling her. She handed over her basket and he weighed the different fruit on his scales, lifting brass weights onto the counterbalance and scribbling the figures on a paper bag. At the last moment, Jameela snatched back one of her father's apples from the scales and replaced it with a ripe peach, drawing an impatient scowl from the stall keeper.

"Any more changes?" he asked gruffly.

Jameela shook her head, blushing. He added up again, then tipped the whole lot into the paper bag, screwed the top tightly and handed it to her. She paid and turned away. Immediately she opened the bag, scooped out the peach and stepped around the stall to the ancient door's steps, just as the little dog moved to sniff at the grimy feet of the beggar boy.

22

Rafiq's eyes flew open when he felt the wet nose against his toes and he kicked out at the mangy mongrel. It yelped and leaped away, looking back reproachfully as the boy blinked bloodshot eyes, taking in the nearby stalls, the bustling crowds, the hot, teeming streets. And, standing next to him, a dark-eyed girl.

He shook his head to clear the sleep that blunted his thinking and sat up quickly, momentarily confused. He rubbed his eyes, but the girl still stood there, an uncertain frown on her face as she stared at the rapidly retreating dog. She gazed at him then, her frown melting away. Silently, she held out her hand. In it was a peach.

Rafiq didn't know what to do. In his uncertainty he felt anger heating his blood. A million thoughts flew through his mind. What trickery was this? He hadn't spoken to anybody for days. He knew no one in this crowded, bustling town. Yet here was this stranger, this girl, handing him sweet fruit. He glanced around suspiciously, but the market was thronged with ordinary shoppers and dealers, strangers who ignored him. And the girl herself didn't appear in any way threatening. She was clearly nothing to do with the authorities.

"Do you want it?" she asked shyly, drawing his attention back to her.

Rafiq faltered, not certain if she were real or part of a forgotten dream, then nodded, hastily wiping his hand on his shirt before reaching out and taking the peach from her palm. It was warm from the sun, or from her touch, and so soft that Rafiq was afraid he'd crush it if he lifted it to his lips. The scent filled him with sunlight and sweetness, sentiments he had forgotten and, to his astonishment, made his eyes brim with unfamiliar tears. Confounded, he blinked them away.

"Thank you," he muttered as he lifted his eyes to her, but the girl had already turned and left him.

Rafiq watched her as she skirted the frenzy of the market. He didn't take his eyes off her as she skipped up the steps of the police station. He gazed at her until she vanished through the swing doors into the lobby. He looked at the warm peach cradled in his hand and smelled its softness and her kindness, and was reluctant to bite into the downy fruit.

In spite of the heat and the noisy activity surrounding him, Rafiq had managed to sleep for several hours.

He leaned back now against the curving stone and let the hand holding the peach drop to his lap as he considered his plans for the day. Although he knew he shouldn't linger, because he had much to do, he remained on the steps, gazing languidly at the busy chowk. He watched the people as they scurried about their business. He looked at their faces as they shouted and laughed and called out. He saw women, some with their faces veiled, and remembered the women in the camp. He saw old men at the stalls and thought of the old man who had brewed their milk tea in the mornings.

Rafiq bit into the peach and paused in his wandering thoughts as the sweetness filled his mouth and the juices slaked his thirst. The girl's image floated in front of his eyes again, teasing his memory, vaguely familiar somehow.

But there was no time for this. Shaking his head with irritation at himself, he spat out the peach stone and the soft memories. He needed to feel the fire in his belly that had driven him to this point, to this retribution. He wanted to feel the heat in his blood and the deep rage that had made him plan his revenge, so that when it was over, he would have the ultimate peace.

But try as he might, all he felt was a vague disquiet which made his muscles heavy and his head ache. He knew what he had to do. He knew that he had to do it. He knew expertly *how* to do it. But it was a struggle. The impetus that had driven him seemed to have been left somewhere in the wild mountains and now he was operating mechanically, without deep passion to fuel him.

Angry with himself, Rafiq scrambled to his feet, turned his back on the chowk and strode to the alley where his horse stood quietly awaiting his return. He led it towards the abandoned site where he had concealed his ammunition, stopping at a street tap to allow the animal to drink from the stone basin. By the time they arrived, the sun was over its peak and just starting to paint shadows on the ground.

There was more activity around the area than the previous night but not enough to concern him. Traffic trundled by on the road and people walked past, gazing at the boy and his horse with nothing more than passing curiosity. Rafiq waited until the street was quiet, then heaved the loose board to one side. He quickly stepped through, dragging the reluctant horse with him, and slid the board back in place so they were out of sight. He crunched his way over the unsteady surface, rocking and sliding where tiles and rubble shifted and slipped. His horse whinnied and jerked its head with fright until they reached where he had hidden the sacks of weapons.

Rafiq checked around him until satisfied no one was watching, then hauled the sacks out, rolled down their tops and examined the contents with grim satisfaction. With extreme care he unpacked them, sorted the explosive materials and prepared them for use. He repacked them in strategic order, positioning trip switches and timing devices at the top of each sack. He armed himself with guns, boxes of bullets and knives, concealing the weaponry beneath his loose clothing. He was ready to fight, should the need arise, but knew it would probably not be necessary.

Solemnly Rafiq heaved the bulging sacks to where his horse stood idly champing weeds. He grunted as he hefted the sacks onto the animal's back and secured them with rope. The horse shied away in protest at the unexpected weight, but Rafiq shouted and jerked it back until it stood passively and allowed itself to be burdened with its deadly load.

23

Jameela picked her way through groups of people sitting on the floor, to where her mother now sat.

"You've moved on a few places," she remarked, squatting down beside her.

Her mother nodded, smiling. "There's been a little progress."

"It's smelly in here after being outside," Jameela whispered, wrinkling up her nose.

"I know," her mother agreed. "There are so many sweaty bodies all squashed together. It's horrible."

They giggled as Jameela put the bag of fruit in her mother's hands. She opened it and looked in.

"You did well," she said, lifting out the apples and peaches, oranges and figs, and examining them for bruises. "Perfect fruit. Not a blemish in sight."

Jameela felt her face warm with pleasure. "And look,

Mamma. These are for us." She showed her the ripe apricots.

Her mother beamed. "I love apricots!"

"I know. That's why I got them."

"How would I manage without you?" her mother asked affectionately.

"Mamma, I gave a peach to a street boy on the steps behind the stall," Jameela said. "He looked so sad and lonely."

"Then it's good that you helped him. We can do without one piece of fruit if it has gone to someone who needs it more."

They settled to enjoy their apricots and her mother told her about the queue moving on, about the new people who had come in, and about how she thought they might be seen soon. Jameela glanced up at the large grimy clock hanging on the wall above the door.

"The day is going so quickly," she said. "I hope it's not much longer."

Her mother nodded and looked towards the counter, where one officer was filling in forms for a young couple with a tiny infant, asleep in its mother's arms.

The second police officer leaned over the counter and gazed around at the expectant crowd. He wiped his hand through his sweaty hair as he too eyed the clock face.

"Who's next?" he called, his voice heavy with fatigue.

To the right of the counter the large family made to get to their feet. There was a very ancient woman among them, with white hair and gnarled hands, who tottered and wobbled as she struggled off the floor. Jameela immediately jumped up to help her. There were also two toddlers, who made a bid for freedom and had to be restrained firmly, whereupon they set up a lusty roar. A heavily pregnant woman with the group got slowly to her feet with the help of the man with her; and all the while, the harassed police officer watched the scene from behind his counter. The attention of the whole room was focused on the activity.

Jameela sat down again and whispered excitedly to her mother, "We're next!"

Her mother smiled, straightening her veil so she would look respectful when she was called to the counter. Jameela could no longer relax and her stomach fluttered. What would they say when called? She glanced towards the clock and watched the minute hand as it clicked forward with the passing time, counting down to the moment when they would find out what had happened to her brother.

And suddenly that moment arrived.

"Next," called the officer as the couple and their baby left the counter.

Jameela felt her heart leap and her fingers tingle as she stood and turned to help her mother to her feet. They approached the police officer, who looked worn out and impatient. Jameela prayed he would have good news for them.

"What can I do for you?" he asked. His voice had a hard edge to it that Jameela heard with dismay.

Her mother spoke for them, but Jameela knew it was difficult for her.

"We want to know…"

Jameela glanced anxiously as her mother hesitated, and then started again.

"We would like to find out about a camp the army found in the mountains. A camp for soldiers … for freedom fighters. We understand there might be boys from the camp here. In the station. My son has been missing for five years. He was taken by them. Is it possible that he is…?"

Her voice faded under the irritated glare of the police officer. He pulled out a sheaf of forms and slapped them on the counter. He snatched up a pen, which he laid on the forms, and looked at them again.

"You need to fill these in."

Her mother paused, then shook her head with shame, dropping her gaze to the counter. "I'm sorry," she said. "It's not possible."

He understood. "Can your daughter complete them?"

Jameela felt a shiver down her spine as she heard herself referred to. She had tried to practise her reading and writing, and could write her name, but lessons had stopped five long years ago. The idea of filling in a detailed form for the police made her insides knot up.

Her mother glanced at her and saw the anxiety in her daughter's face. "No. I'm sorry. We need help," she replied, her voice firmer as she turned back to the police officer.

He nodded, accustomed to this response from women,

and swivelled the forms to his side of the counter. Completing them wasn't as arduous as they had thought, and once he understood they were alone and needed assistance, he appeared to soften. They proceeded through standard questions about their personal information and details of the enquiry. The officer then stamped and signed the forms, and asked them to put their mark on them, before disappearing into the back of the station.

Once they were alone, Jameela turned to her mother, her face pale with worry. "What happens now?" she whispered.

Her mother met her eye. "I don't know, child. We find out about who is here, I suppose."

They waited in silence. It was several minutes before the officer returned. He stood in front of them and his eyes were kind, but sad, and Jameela knew the news wasn't good before he even opened his mouth.

"There *was* a camp in the mountains, run by militants," he started, then took a deep breath. "There were boys there of all ages. Men too, and women. When the army invaded it, it was at night. There was a dust storm and it was dark."

He paused and Jameela's breath caught in her throat.

"I'm sorry, but there were no survivors."

The fist of desolation that gripped her heart made her limbs suddenly weak. Beside her, her mother gasped, her hands flying to her face. Instinctively Jameela put her arm round her mother's trembling shoulders. Her thoughts were a whirl, when through the sickening feeling, the officer's voice emerged.

"...don't have the names of those in the camp. It is possible that your son wasn't there. Was never there. He could be somewhere else. Somewhere safe."

Jameela knew the officer was trying to be kind, trying to protect them from the grief that was swamping her, but he really could not help them. He was just saying words, comforting words that were meaningless.

Her mother spoke then, her voice a soft whisper.

"We heard there were boys ... a boy. Captured. Held here. Perhaps... Maybe he might..." Her voice weakened, trailed away.

But the officer shook his head. "There's nobody here, madam." He looked away, did not meet their eyes. "There were no survivors from the camp." He glanced back again. "But if we find anything that might help you, we have your details." He patted the forms they had completed, indicating that he was drawing their time at the counter to a close.

"What else can we do?" her mother asked.

The officer smiled sympathetically and shrugged his shoulders. "Keep looking. Anywhere and everywhere you can think of. And pray."

They turned away from the counter.

"I wish you good fortune in your search," was his parting comment.

Nodding their thanks, they slowly made their way to

the door. Jameela couldn't believe that it was all over; that they had travelled all this way to speak to the authorities and still had no information about the whereabouts of Rafiq. Her feet were difficult to move, as though the floor were sticky, and she was afraid to look at her mother. She felt as though all the strength and hope inside her had instantly drained away, leaving an empty fragile shell that might shatter at any moment. Tears trembled on her lashes as they stood together on the top step of the police station, uncertain of what to do, where to go. Her mother ran her hands distractedly through her hair, her fingers fretting at the hem of her veil.

"We'd better make our way back to the bus station," she finally uttered, her voice cracking slightly.

Jameela nodded, not trusting herself to speak.

"We'll buy some rice flour and perhaps a pretty scarf for Afrah first."

Jameela knew her mother was trying to be strong, trying not to let the news drag her further down than she already was.

"And we'll visit the White Mosque to pray."

"What are we praying for?" Jameela asked bleakly.

Her mother looked at her sharply. "To find your brother. And to give thanks for not having received worse news."

24

The mosaic steps of the White Mosque gleamed brightly in the sun. They were hot underfoot and, in spite of the toughness of his feet, Rafiq curled his toes as he climbed to the top. He hung his head, gazing at the designs on the floor, distracted by the myriad of tiny tiles that made up the complex twisting patterns. Slowly he lifted his head and looked up at the dazzling whiteness of the imposing edifice that reached skywards. The white marble against the aching blue expanse of sky reminded him of the snowy summits of the Pir Panjals, and desolation surged through his body as he thought of his lost mountain home. For the second time that day, he felt salt tears stinging his eyes and he rubbed his hand across his grimy face, leaving a streak of clean.

Turning from the source of his confusion, Rafiq glanced to check that his laden horse was still safely tethered at the bottom of the steps. He squatted down to review his plans, staring grimly across the chowk at his target: the police station.

Standing on its steps were two figures. Rafiq screwed his eyes up in the sunshine and recognized one of them as the girl from earlier that morning. Once again, her appearance nudged something deep in his memory, disturbing his focus. He recalled the rare kindness she had shown to him and the sweetness of her manner, then frowned when he remembered that she had not even heard his muttered thanks. She was talking to an old woman – her mother? – dipping her head to better listen to what was being said. Moments later they descended the steps together.

Rafiq's quick eye couldn't help but notice that the girl's movements lacked the sprightliness of that morning, when she had skittered up the steps of the police station like a kid goat. This time her limbs seemed slow and heavy, like his own. The girl and the woman mingled with the crowds of shoppers in the market. Rafiq stood on his tiptoes, but they had melted into the throng and he couldn't spot them among the bobbing heads.

He turned and entered the mosque to pray before his mission, trying to gather his drifting thoughts together once more. His mind hardened and chilled to its purpose; but one tiny part of him flushed with warmth, like a glowing ember in a dying fire, because he knew the girl was no longer in the police station.

25

Jameela lingered listlessly as her mother rummaged among the racks of scarves suspended above women's hijabs and skirts in the centre of the market. The helpful owner pulled the racks down so that dozens of shimmering scarves cascaded over the counter.

"Help me choose, Jameela," her mother said. "Moping won't make Rafiq come back, and we are no worse off today than we were yesterday."

Jameela knew her mother was right, but was finding it impossible to shake off her misery when she had built up this single day to mean so much. Her mother turned to her, dropping the scarves on the counter.

"Look at me, Jameela," she ordered, snatching up her daughter's limp hand. "Look at me."

Jameela lifted her downcast eyes and her mother saw the shining tears and felt her heart breaking for her daughter. But she had to be firm.

"What did you truly believe would happen today? Did you think we would be going home with Rafiq sitting between us on the village bus? Do I really have such a foolish daughter? Did you honestly believe that we'd find him waiting for us in the police station? That we'd bring him home with us tonight like a bag of fresh fruit or a new scarf?"

Jameela shook her head. Her mother's words made her feel childish. She didn't know what to say. But no matter: her mother had plenty to say for both of them.

"We can't let this sadness take us over, Jameela. We have to be strong, have to keep hoping, to continue moving forward. For five years I have been living with this heart-break deep inside here." She pounded her chest with her closed fist. "I would not have survived if I had let every scrap of disappointing news extinguish my hope. Something in our dreams drew us here today; we cannot lose sight of that. Today has some meaning for us, although we don't know it yet. But we will not go home with our hearts heavy and our hopes broken."

Jameela spoke softly. "You're right. I don't believe that he is dead," she said, shaking her head. "His spirit is too strong. I'll try, Mamma."

Her mother smiled at her. "Good girl. We need to believe in something. We will get through this together."

She turned back to the stall and picked up the discarded scarves. "Now, let's choose something to keep little Afrah happy after her hard work caring for your father and the boys."

But Jameela didn't answer. Nor was she next to her mother at the stall.

Her mother turned to see what had distracted the child now. Jameela was standing a little way off, her back to the stall, her back to her mother. She was facing the White Mosque, behind which the sun was shining brightly. But it was clear that she wasn't looking at it. Instead she was looking at someone moving through the crowd, someone her mother couldn't yet see. Was it one of the village women? She stepped closer to her daughter, eager to join in any local banter.

But then she saw the stranger; or rather his silhouette. He had stopped a few paces in front of Jameela. From his outline her mother could see it was a boy, a little taller than her daughter, leading a heavily laden horse by a rope. Jameela seemed to know him. And as her mother watched, the sun gilded their dark silhouettes with a line of shining brightness.

Her breath stopped in her throat. The scene seared into her thoughts, blazing through her memory. And it seemed she was gazing at a tableau from years ago, from a familiar courtyard in a distant village played by identical characters, but so dissimilar and displaced from the here and now that she was unable to make sense of what her eyes saw and what her thoughts told her.

For that was how she had last seen them together.

On that final golden evening.

Her heart froze. The blood drained from her face. The coloured scarf, still caught between her fingers, drifted to the ground, where it rested, limp and soft. She was unable to move, unable to tear her eyes from where Jameela and the boy stood.

Time slowed until it stopped. The chaotic colours of the market faded about her. The bustle of the crowds dissolved into silence.

At that instant, everything vanished except for her daughter and the boy, who stood out with startling clarity. Jameela, in her conversation with this stranger, stepped slightly to one side, blocking the brilliance of the sun so that their silhouettes melted back into colour and detail, every movement seeming to happen with deliberate slowness. The girl's foot took for ever to lift from the dust and press down again into its new position on the soft surface. Her watching mother saw the folds of her daughter's cotton dress alter and reshape to the new tensions on them. Jameela shifted her weight and slowly, slowly, lifted her hand to her scarf, drawing it towards the front of her head. The glossy threads gleamed under the hot sun.

And because time had stopped, her confused mother saw all these things in minute detail and considered them with wonder. Now the boy stranger was clearly visible to her. She saw his smeared skin, his long hair, his ragged clothes. His dark eyes. His familiar face…

On recognizing him, she felt the blood rush back to her

body in a sudden flood that left her weak and light-headed, staggering against the counter. The universe shifted and time surged back to its usual pace, accompanied by a wave of deafening sounds, sickening smells and dizzying colours.

The market exploded, jangling and jarring into her awareness; and the next thing she knew, she was sitting in an untidy heap on the ground, Jameela beside her, fanning her hot face, asking again and again if she was all right. She nodded, although Jameela's voice seemed to come from some great distance, accompanied by a persistent echo that forced her mother to frown as she struggled to understand the words.

The stall keeper rushed over with a glass of water, which she took gratefully and drank down. She looked at Jameela, her eyes wild, her hand pointing frantically towards where her daughter had been standing with the boy. She tried to speak, to explain what she had seen – *whom* she had seen – but her lips would not cooperate with her hurtling thoughts and her utterances made no sense, which frustrated her further.

Jameela held her hand gently and explained what she thought her mother wanted to hear.

"It was the boy I gave the peach to earlier today. You remember? The street boy? I told you. He saw me as he crossed the chowk. He came over to thank me." She glanced behind her, towards the police station. "He has business there too," she said, turning back to her mother. "I know he shouldn't have come up to me like he did, a stranger in the market, but I remembered him from this morning, so it wasn't as disrespectful as you think."

But her mother shook her head and croaked in a distressed way that immediately had Jameela up and looking for more water from the stall keeper. When she turned back, her mother was on her feet, stumbling towards the police station, where the boy was now struggling up the steps with two sacks unloaded from his horse.

Her mother stood at the bottom and stared up at him. She summoned all her strength to cry out a single word to the retreating street boy.

"Rafiq!"

And Jameela stared at her in utter shock as the desperate cry soared upwards.

26

Rafiq froze mid-step when he heard his name being called. Nobody had uttered it since the terrible night of the sandstorm, when Ahmed had hammered on the door of his hut and shouted for him to come and help. His name had been lost that night, along with his spirit; and now, in this town of strangers, somebody had found it again and was calling to him. And his name sounded safe in that person's mouth; Rafiq did not feel threatened as he lowered his lethal sacks to the ground and slowly turned to see who knew him.

At the bottom of the steps was an old woman staring up at him, leaning over as she grasped the railing for support, his name fading from her lips. Behind her was the girl. Rafiq recalled that they were together. But how did the woman know his name?

He remained beside his weapons and gazed down, his

face impassive. Perhaps she was acting on the orders of another. His heart leaped as he thought that there could be other freedom fighters lurking among the crowds in the chowk. Perhaps he had been wrong all along, and some of his brothers had escaped the attack on the camp. Perhaps he was not alone. Perhaps this one final assignment could be delayed.

His bright eyes flickered around the market, seeking any other faces turned towards him or watching him with more than idle interest. Even if he didn't recognize them, he would be able to identify them instantly as one of his own. A quick blaze of his true spirit flashed in him again as he swiftly searched the masses of people. His gaze lit on a group of men at the rear of a stall, but he lost interest as soon as they burst out laughing and slapped each other on the back. No true freedom fighter would behave in such a manner in a public place. Then there was the man picking his teeth at the side of the police station. He was looking up at Rafiq, but the boy saw no glimmer of acknowledgement, just casual passing interest. The two men leaving the chowk? But they turned away, deep in conversation, when Rafiq looked at them.

His hope dwindled when he saw no evidence of other fighters. These were just ordinary shoppers. Rafiq felt cheated.

His face hardened as he returned his gaze to the old woman. She was clearly acting independently. Her features were vaguely familiar, but he didn't know her from this town. Her familiarity came to his memory from another time, another place. Images flashed in his head, but didn't endure long enough for him to search them, to make sense of them.

He felt irritation bubbling through his veins as his fragile concentration fractured. He struggled to keep his mind on the task at hand, reminding himself that he was a soldier, a Kashmiri freedom fighter, a true warrior who was not distracted by old women and young girls. He had to avenge the deaths of his brothers and he could delay no longer.

The girl had moved quietly up the steps and now stood just beneath him.

"Are you Rafiq?" she asked, her voice soft and hesitant, her eyes searching his face. "Are you my brother?"

And now it was his turn to hesitate. There was much to consider before he could answer such questions, but his mind would not be still. Already he had put himself in great danger: bristling with weapons, his hand resting on a sack of explosives, standing on the steps of a police station. And now this woman, this girl, bringing his name back to him at his moment of retribution. What was happening?

A soldier must remember the hazards lurking round every corner when carrying out a mission, he reminded himself. "Strike and leave," Kareem had warned repeatedly. "Keep your needs at bay," Abdullah had told them until they were weary of the words.

But still he hesitated, looking at the girl, because what

she asked had already reached deep inside him. What would it mean if he answered? Would he still be a true soldier of Kashmir – or just a village boy?

This was a line he had crossed before; he wondered if he could cross it again. And although he didn't know it yet, in a forgotten corner of Rafiq's heart, a tiny spark flickered to life.

"Yes," he found himself replying. "My name is Rafiq."

JANE MITCHELL lives in Dublin. She has worked as a teacher, and with young offenders and young adults with physical disabilities. Her previous novels include *When Stars Stop Spinning*, winner of the Bisto Book of the Year Award.

Jane has travelled extensively through India and Nepal, where she was struck by the responsibilities placed upon children; she saw girls as young as eight caring for babies and siblings, working in the fields or serving in markets. Boys worked on the railways, washed clothes and cooked food at street stalls. Most of these children did not have the chance to attend school.

Chalkline is set in Kashmir, situated in the northernmost corner of India, in the Himalayan mountains. It is a territory disputed by India, China and Pakistan, and armed conflict is common throughout the region. Amnesty International reports that armed factions have recruited and used children in their hostilities. Most of these children have no choice; they fight to survive.

Rafiq could be one of them.

www.janemitchell.ie

Amnesty International

Amnesty International is a movement of ordinary people from across the world standing up for humanity and human rights. Our purpose is to protect individuals wherever justice, fairness, freedom and truth are denied.

Worldwide, hundreds of thousands of young people under eighteen, like Rafiq, have been affected by armed conflict. They are recruited into government armed forces, paramilitaries, civil militia and other armed groups. Often they are abducted at school, on the streets or at home. Others enlist "voluntarily", usually because they see few alternatives. They endure experiences like those of Rafiq and the other child soldiers in *Chalkline*.

This happens even though the UN Convention on the Rights of the Child does not allow the participation in armed conflict of children aged under eighteen.

Amnesty International is a member of the Coalition to Stop the Use of Child Soldiers, and we work to end the recruitment of children into armed forces and to reintegrate former child soldiers back into civilian life.

Youth groups

We have an active membership of over 550 youth groups in the UK. Youth groups are gatherings of young people in schools, sixth form colleges or youth clubs who meet to campaign f or Amnesty International. They hold publicity stunts, write letters to go vernment leaders and officials, fund-raise, get publicity in their local paper, hold assemblies and create displays. You can also join as an individual member and receiv e magazines and letter-writing actions.

If you would like to join Amnesty International, join or set up a youth group, or simply find out more, go to www.amnesty.org.uk/youth

Amnesty International UK, The Human Rights Action Centre, 17–25 New Inn Yard, London EC2A 3EA 020 7033 1596 student@amnesty.org.uk www.amnesty.org.uk

---

"I would like you to give a message. Please do your best to tell the w orld what is happening to us, the children. So that other children don't ha ve to pass through this violence."
A fifteen-year-old girl, speaking to Amnesty International in Uganda.

She was forcibly abducted at night from her home b y the Lord's Resistance Army (LRA), an armed opposition movement fighting the Ugandan government. She was made to kill a boy who tried to escape. She saw another boy being hacked to death for not raising the alarm when a friend ran away. She was beaten when she dropped a water container and ran for cover under gunfire. She received thirty-five days of military training and was sent to fight the go vernment army.

Life is harsh in the mountain village in Nepal where Lakshmi works hard alongside her mother to look after the family. When her stepfather finds her a job as a maid in the city, Lakshmi begins the long journey to India dreaming of earning money and making her family proud.

The truth that awaits her is a living nightmare.

"An unforgettable account of sexual slavery as it exists now."

Booklist

US National Book Award Finalist

BY PATRICIA McCORMICK